T0270411

Honeymoons in Temporary Locations

Also by Ashley Shelby
Published by the University of Minnesota Press

South Pole Station

HONEYMOONS IN TEMPORARY LOCATIONS

Ashley Shelby

University of Minnesota Press
Minneapolis
London

"Muri" was first published by Radix Media as part of its Futures Science Fiction series.

Published by the University of Minnesota Press
111 Third Avenue South, Suite 290
Minneapolis, MN 55401-2520
http://www.upress.umn.edu

ISBN 978-1-5179-1707-4 (hc)
ISBN 978-1-5179-1871-2 (pb)

Library of Congress record available at https://lccn.loc.gov/2024002499

Printed in Canada on acid-free paper

The University of Minnesota is an equal-opportunity educator and employer.

32 31 30 29 28 27 26 25 24   10 9 8 7 6 5 4 3 2 1

For Hudson and Joey

Within a few weeks now Draba, the smallest flower that blows, will sprinkle every sandy place with small blooms. He who hopes for spring with upturned eye never sees so small a thing as Draba. He who despairs of spring with downcast eye steps on it, unknowing. He who searches for spring with his knees in the mud finds it, in abundance. . . . After all it is no spring flower, but only a postscript to a hope.

—ALDO LEOPOLD, *A SAND COUNTY ALMANAC*

Contents

ORAL HISTORY

3 Muri

34 Honeymoons in Temporary Locations

DOCUMENTS (RECOVERED)

53 Post-Impact Craigslist Ads

57 Impact Cruises' Brochure Text: "Endangered Cities 7-Day Free-Sail Cruise"

59 Unicorn Investments Newsletter: Subscription Confirmation E-mail

62 Three Rivers Park District Class Description: "New Friends at the Feeder"

64 "Incident on Yellowstone Trail": Climate Crime Files Podcast, Episode 276

74 Federal Eligibility Questionnaire from the Temporary Aid to Climate-Impacted Deserving Poor Benefits Program

77 Ersatz Café Menu (Store #350)

81 Violent Biophilia in Solastalgia Patients: Case Study

86 Climafeel In-House Marketing Brief: [Vortex Biologics]

PARTICIPANT HISTORIES FROM THE CLIMAFEEL CLINICAL TRIAL

95 The Ingenious Futility of Warblers (Elizabeth Fugit)

102 They Don't Tell You Where to Put the Pain (Winfield Scott)

116 Your Ghost Remains Upright (Deacon Kompkoff-Blackwood)

123 The Sickness (Santiago Faucheaux)

141 "Mark"

145 Acknowledgments

ORAL HISTORY

MURI

*Yes, this is a strange craft; a strange history, too,
and strange folks on board.*

— HERMAN MELVILLE, *BENITO CERENO*

1

It had long been whispered that the job we were only the latest to undertake turned sane men into lunatics. They returned as babbling idiots who never again stepped foot on an ice-breaking bulker. Not that they didn't try. The pay was commensurate with the danger of the job, so they would shed identities and buy new ones in order to do the run again. Disturbed men can, of course, become synthetically sane for short periods of time; inevitably, though, the adhesive that binds the mask degrades and then the game is up. If they talked, they were visited, and if, after the visits, they continued to talk, they disappeared.

The run is straightforward: from the marshy port of Iqaluit through Frobisher Bay, we coast down the Labrador Current and shimmy though the Strait of Belle Isle before curving east through Cabot Strait, and then sail the familiar Atlantic waters off the east coast of the United States, cruise around the Lesser Antilles, almost hoping for pirates off the coasts of Guyana and Brazil who might mistake us for a regular cargo ship, with a stop in Ushuaia before we cross the Drake Passage to land that cargo on the Antarctic coast. The stakes are as high as the pay: a captain who fails to complete the run is, by contract and with his full agreement, remanded to the Federal Corrective Training Settlement, a maritime reeducation camp with no publicly known address. By another name, it is banishment.

There have been many explanations for the difficulties experienced by the men who've been on this run: some argue that it's the sulfate aerosol veil that hangs over each Pole—the reflective particles disturb the mind. Others claim the men must have stared into the geo-engineered albedo without their eclipse glasses, damaging their vision and leading them to see things that are not there. Still others assume the crews' strange behavior is the result of the crushing stress of dealing with the Russian threat; their nuclear subs prowl the Arctic planting flags on the sea floor. Some say it is the nature of the operation itself that addles men's minds.

The project had been ongoing for two years without detection by the public. Sure, there had been rumors and warnings from conspiracy theorists who, in this profoundly changed world, were sometimes closer to the truth than even they might believe. However, there could be no mistaking that the animals were disappearing from the region even more rapidly than expected.

Two weeks before I was given command of the *Precession,* an optimally manned polar class 2 icebreaker, the Intergovernmental Assisted Colonization Program publicly announced the successful relocation of the Western Hudson Bay Group, acknowledging for the first time the operation's existence. This was met with a resurgence of panic and Impact-related angst, except among the First Nation peoples still trying to hack out a living on the spindly fringes of the Arctic. They had already known of the relocations—were the first to know—and had provided practical knowledge and aid, despite their misgivings. (There had been no need for NDAs. Although the indigenous population had been the Paul Reveres of Impact, they had, of course, been ignored. We understood, as they did, too, that if they were to talk about the Relocation project, they would be ignored again.)

Within days, however, public sentiment shifted in favor of moving the bears from the Arctic to the Antarctic—to most people the two landscapes were interchangeable. Biologists remained apoplectic. It was "an inversion of the accepted principles of natural biodiversity," a rich accusation coming from individuals who had supported the creation of Styrofoam floes in the Barents Sea and airdrops of "bear chow" on Ellesmere Island. Their version of natural biodiversity resulted in large swaths of western Canada crawling with grizzly mamas nursing polar bear cubs, thanks to their short-lived frozen embryo transplant project. (I quickly came to believe scientists have no useful role in post-Impact logistics.)

The pod I was charged with transporting from Iqaluit to the Weddell Sea was the last group of polar bears known to be living in the Arctic regions outside of Russia, which refused to participate in the project. These were Baffin Bay bears—the ones who had initially been the hardest to capture but who subsequently became, due to starvation and physical weakness, as docile as dogs.

As the master of the last icebreaker to leave the Arctic with ursine cargo, I underwent special firearms and Large Mammal Animal Training, despite the fact that we'd be traveling with several biologists and a large-animal handler and a vet and the beasts would never leave their steel enclosures located in the hangar off the operation deck.

I also underwent counseling during which I was told about this lunacy specific to the Iqaluit run, which manifested itself as hallucinations—even mass hysteria—featuring one common theme: the bears speak. Not in husky-like complaints but in English, with clear diction and a slight but very strange accent. I was shown film of exit interviews given by the crew of the infamous *Marigold* immediately after they landed at Ushuaia, conducted in a secure facility. The crew maintained that not only did the bears communicate in English, several bears had acted as Able Seamen, capable of performing routine duties, such as taking on lookout shifts and anchor watch. A deck cadet claimed, with a straight face, that a seven-hundred-pound female called Nuna could execute rudder orders. It was on this run, undertaken before the social media clampdown, that one of the petty officers managed to record a short video with his Device. It was widely dismissed as a deepfake. After that, shipboard communication technology was put under lock and key. Devices were not permitted on board and the satellite phone was accessible only by the Master, the Chief Officer, and the Chief Engineer. Photos no longer hit social media.

Most on board the *Marigold*—and the *Precession,* for that matter—remembered pre-Impact. We were children when things were growing strange. Though we had been protected from the worst disasters, occurring mostly in the global south, we were habituated early to a certain constant low-grade anxiety in adults that found its core outside rather than within. This, we were told later, was different. Things hadn't always been like this. We had been taught that anxiety was nearly always based on imaginary fears, found mainly in people who had little to be afraid of and who therefore manufactured fear themselves. With the advent of "reality-based fear," the kind that germinates in war zones, came deep—bone-deep—sorrow that even children could not misunderstand. How do you explain to a child who has never experienced the normal contours of spring why many adults preferred death than a world without it?

When the old men and women began to die off, there was even less fear, but there was more anger. Sometimes it seemed the anger would overwhelm us all. Sometimes the anger warped perceptions. Under certain conditions, the human mind can, like tectonic plates under pressure, undergo cataclysmic shifts. With each slip of the plates and the brutal chafing that resulted, sanity begins to lose its absolute definition. It's difficult to understand the nature of reality when you stand with one foot in a vanished world and the other in chaos.

Shortly after that run, the crew of the *Marigold* was dispatched on a classified assignment in the Southern Ocean—rumored to be where the reeducation camp was located on a nameless island—and subsequently disappeared. No other crew spoke of talking bears after that, but no crew did the same run twice. I vowed I was not going to become one of the lunatics, the fatwood that would spark a conflagration. I was determined to complete this final run without incident. It was for this reason that I said nothing the first time Muri spoke to me.

2

We'd set sail from Iqaluit on May 20 on the *Precession,* bound for the Polar Wildlife Relocation Hub on the northwest coast of Antarctica. Like the crews before us, we were armed with four etorphine-loaded tranqs and two .375 American Safari Magnums (motto: Any game shot with an American Safari Magnum stays shot.) Because the Arctic, in addition to becoming liquid, had grown increasingly lawless, each relocation vessel also contained six 9mm semiautomatic handguns. Previous boats had been harassed by Russian nuclear submarines patrolling the Lomonosov Ridge, but there had never been any open confrontation.

Around three a.m. on the third day, after we'd successfully navigated the Labrador Current and were edging around the Lower Savage Islands in the Gabriel Strait, the large-animal trainer entered the enclosure of a bear she believed to be sick to the point of unconsciousness. It killed her immediately. This bear also fatally mauled the boatswain, who'd come running when he'd heard the zookeeper's screams. Because of the hour, because of the distance between the berthing and the livestock containment area, and because our onboard CCTV had gone offline as we passed through the dead zone off Avingasiltuit Siginirsipangat Island in the Labrador Sea, none of us realized what had happened until daybreak, when the bears began lumbering up from the cargo hold onto the deck.

I was shaken awake by my second mate so violently that I fell from my berthing. His face was pale as the moon and I read in it the kind of terror that sees no way out. At my prompting, he tried to speak but could not. I dressed quickly and followed him to the Zodiac deck. There I observed a scene of such brutality that the edges of the memory have curled inward, obscuring everything but the slick pools of blood and the red-stained coats of two large bears. These animals flanked a much smaller bear the crew had named Winky, but whom I would later know as Muri, the most remarkable animal I've ever known. He was undersized and thin, but the other bears moved downwind from him when he passed, some even turning aside to avoid accidental eye contact. His sentries, on the other hand, who were clearly under his command, were the kind of terrifying ice-beasts whose distant roars caused many an Arctic explorer to soil himself.

Five bodies lay before me, dead, torn apart. I recognized the red boots of a young engine tech from Sacramento, as well as the cerulean blue parka of one of the biologists. The rest were too badly mutilated for quick identification. To my dismay, I was unable to keep from vomiting, and the puddle of bile threw off a cloud of steam. Behind Muri, two other bears paced but made no further moves toward my men, who, I now noticed, were conspicuously unarmed and who were trying to disappear behind the crane. Two were sitting in the unlaunched Zodiac. They looked like children.

It seemed very important to make no decisive movements. The bears, agitated though they were, watched us closely, waiting for us to make the first move. My second, a Chilean named Wagner, trembled next to me, his hysteria barely contained, and I saw that he too was unarmed. "Why haven't these animals been tranquilized?" I asked quietly.

"The guns," he replied, his breathing labored. "They're gone, sir."

"Gone?"

"Overboard."

I examined his face. His eyes were bloodshot and widened with panic; his neck gaiter was heavily frosted at the mouth. He slapped at his thighs over and over again with his heavy mittens, and I soon realized he was, in this foolish manner, trying to steady his legs.

"Who threw them overboard?"

Wagner turned his eyes to the bears but quickly redirected them to his boots.

"Who?" I barked.

"They did, sir."

I knew the next words I spoke to my second had to be measured; I needed to inoculate the rest of the crew against this contagious hysteria. "It doesn't matter how they got overboard. What matters now is that we get the animals back into the hold."

Muri and the other bears continued watching me with their buckshot-dark eyes. The two bears standing on either side of Muri— I couldn't help but think of them as bodyguards—began panting. The largest one hauled himself on his hind legs. He was a magnificent creature, kingly in bearing and easily ten feet tall. Now it was my turn to try to control my trembling legs. Feigning interest in the horizon I tried to collect myself. "Where is the rest of the livestock crew?"

"No one has been able to find them, sir," Wagner replied. He hesitated. "Messersmith says he saw Marshall jump overboard."

Behind Muri's sentries came five more bears from below, blinking and sneezing, sniffing the glossy blood on the deck. One who tried to lap at the blood received a quick bite on the shoulder from Muri. My eyes turned to the body closest to me—the engine tech who had been repairing a leaky seal in the propeller room the last time I'd seen him. Muri and I locked eyes. Strangely, I was overwhelmed by the feeling I was in no immediate peril, so long as I didn't try anything unexpected. As if reading my mind, Muri barked at a dun-colored bear who had just emerged from the hold. After a moment of ursine cogitation, the bear gently picked up the dead crewman between its teeth, walked over to the starboard side, got up on its hind legs, and dropped the body over the side of the ship. Over the next three minutes, this undertaker effected a sea burial for each of the slain. Next to me, Wagner covered his face with his hands.

Muri conferred with a bear even thinner than he was, one probably too old to have been taken on this journey and who should've been left to starve. After reaching some kind of understanding, the subaltern lumbered up the deck stairs and toward the bridge. Muri began moving toward me. I felt no physical, visceral fear as Muri approached—again, I was somehow reassured that I was not yet in danger of losing my life, that I was required for Muri's plans in a way others were not. However, I was enveloped by heavy dread. I remained rooted to the deck when Muri stopped a few feet from me and hauled himself onto his hind legs, his dirty paws hanging at his sides.

The words, when they came, were hyponasal and accent-inflected. But they were unmistakably English: "Let us meet in the Navigation Room, Captain."

Only Wagner's reaction suggested that I was not hallucinating. He scrambled backwards, colliding with the foot of the crane, and began fumbling for something in his pocket, which I hoped was a gun. Instead, he pulled out an illegal cell phone that must have been overlooked during the X-ray and pat-down. With tremulous fingers, he held the phone out toward Muri as if it were a talisman that could make the animal disappear.

"Latufa," Muri said, inclining his head toward the larger of his bodyguards. Latufa, who—and it can only be described in these terms—tended to the wizened, elderly bear who had been the last to emerge from enclosures, left off his ministrations and loped down the deck toward Wagner. The other crewmen scattered, but my second remained paralyzed. Latufa stopped short just before reaching us, skidding a little on the wet deck.

"Give him the phone," Muri said to Wagner.

Wagner could not speak. Latufa crept toward him, and I felt my throat begin to constrict with panic. Still standing, Muri addressed me. "Captain, perhaps he waits for your command."

"Do as he says, Wagner."

Slowly, Wagner turned to look behind him, into the dark waters of the Labrador Sea, then back at the bears. "Do it now."

Wagner looked at me. "It's okay," I said. After one more glance over his shoulder, he fell into a crouch and placed his phone on the deck. He sent it skidding toward Latufa, who caught it under his paw.

Muri fell from his full height back to all fours. "Come, let us talk. Your crew will remain safe so long as they follow instructions."

As he spoke these words, bears began closing in on my crew, rounding them up like sheep.

3

Contagious diseases of the mind breed on beams of light. They travel on the wings of thought. Or perhaps they are propagated by a mysterious hand that sows haphazardly. These strange harvests have occurred with some frequency throughout human history, and yet they have never become fully part of that history. Like half-formed relics, they're set at the margins of collective experience, halfway between real and imaginary. Certainly, they are "real" in some ways. The hundreds of men and women who danced the St. Vitus Dance in fifteenth-century Strasbourg—commanded by some unknown pestilential compulsion—and died in blood-soaked shoes were real enough; their corpses did not disintegrate like a dream upon waking but were carried, intact, to the burial ground. The streets of Metz were actually filled with 1,100 dancers along with musicians hired by desperate city fathers in the hopes that the afflicted would exhaust themselves more quickly with song. Those dancing spoke of being immersed in a stream of blood, which obliged them to leap and contort their bodies in order to escape. This perception was passed on, again and again, silently, from person to person, city to city, until, like a cloud pulled apart by the wind, the madness dissolved.

While moralists view these contagions as examples of human frailty, other more pragmatic and generous minds might examine the state of the society that farrowed such maladies. One might even ask whether they are, in fact, the offspring of the ages in which they appeared. If that is, indeed, the case, then you may understand why I accepted that what was happening was real and not the product of a diseased mind. In such an existence, animals will talk. They will tell you their grievances and you will listen, as I did. This is why I followed Muri to the bridge.

The Navigation Room was still bathed in red light as I'd left it the night before, but I saw at once that most of our communications panels were dark. The third mate was nowhere to be seen. I walked over to the windows. On the starboard side, sunrays dusted the horizon. Below us, the water was still bergy—freely navigable but not entirely absent of glacier ice. I also observed it had begun to take on an oily appearance—a slushiness that consisted of needle-like spicules and amorphous ice. This, along with the obvious sign of the rising sun on our right, indicated that we were heading back north and perhaps had been for some time. It troubled me greatly that I had not noticed the turn. It was only later that I wondered if perhaps I had not wanted to.

I sat down heavily on one of the chairs and looked at the bear Muri.

"You will return this ship to Frobisher Bay," he said.

After a moment, during which I struggled to understand his meaning, I laughed. "Impossible."

"Captain, you will forgive me if I point out that you don't seem to have a firm grasp on what is either possible or impossible."

I marveled at Muri's speech momentarily, but just as two foreigners fall easily into lingua franca without stopping to ask how fluency was achieved, we pressed forward with the urgent matters at hand.

"We have neither enough provision nor enough fuel," I lied.

"The ship was set on a course for Antarctica. The itinerary noted no refueling stops."

"Well, the ship's deviation has certainly already been noted by the Coast Guard."

Muri seemed at this moment almost to smile. "Your bluff fails. I know what happened to your Coast Guard. These are piratical waters now."

I thought of the young comms tech, Messersmith, who should've been stationed on the bridge at the time of the revolt. Could he have called it in before being dragged off? How, I wondered, would he have characterized our emergency? *The bears have escaped. The bears have taken over the ship. The bears speak. The bears know the lay of the changed land better than we do.*

I decided to try reason. "If you know what happened to the Coast Guard, then surely you know what has happened to the Arctic." For the first time Muri averted his eyes. I decided to press my advantage. "It is dying. It is practically ice-free. You'll survive in Antarctica. There's plenty of prey."

"You really insist on redesigning the entire biota of earth, don't you?"

"Excuse me?"

"Yes, we have heard the promises. We will feast upon the penguins and seals unaccustomed to predators. And we'll wipe them from the face of the continent. What then?"

"If you stay in Baffin Bay, you won't make it. This buys you time."

"Time cannot be bought, Captain. This is a lie you men feast upon while we die. Unlike you, we understand our predicament. We will either fade from Earth in unfamiliar territory or we will do it at home. Ask yourself how you'd prefer to die."

I could think of no response, and we sat in silence for some moments.

"Where's Messermith?" I finally asked. "My communications specialist."

"The young man on the bridge? He is alive, though I imagine he will now be of little use to you."

"What does that mean?"

"The human tongue is plump and flexible, nothing like ours, which requires much training to produce even the simplest word. I can only imagine how difficult it would be for a man to speak without one."

Again, I was saturated with dread. "You've disabled the navigation system. Do you expect me to navigate without my instruments?"

"You have a compass and you were surely not allowed to board a ship without knowing how to navigate by dead reckoning."

"A commander never willingly yields power over his vessel."

"Then do it willingly."

Latufa appeared at the door, unable to advance farther into the room due to his massive shoulders. "There's one other thing," Muri said. "They want to hunt."

"That cannot happen."

A rough, sandy series of barks that suggested laughter shook me. Muri placed his paw on a navigation chart that had been unrolled onto the chart table. He indicated that I should approach. Under one of his rust-brown claws lay the Newfoundland/Labrador Coast. I knew from earlier readings that we were heading toward Edgell Island, a barren, uninhabitable rock north of Resolution Island. The terminal melt of the Greenland Ice Sheet meant that the loose-ice areas where bearded seals could be found were rarer than functioning coal mines and that anchoring in a slushy latitude was an exercise in futility, but Muri was insistent. "They will not hear of moving on without an opportunity to hunt." He glanced over at Latufa, who was huffing now, his obsidian tongue drooped over a yellowed canine. "Even now they are restless and mutinous. Latufa's mother will not eat the chow and she grows weaker by the hour."

"You haven't a chance of achieving your objective. Help will come for us."

Muri considered me for a moment. I was startled to see his heretofore impenetrable black eyes laughing. "You won't call it in."

"Why would you think I wouldn't?"

"Captain, the run has failed. Some may wonder if you weren't somehow complicit in the failure."

He gave me a fragment of time to recall the probable outcome of my return to shore—an outcome that would commence immediately, regardless if the bears were onboard when I was rescued. Each aspect of this unspeakable truth sliced at a different angle.

My silence indicated to Muri assent. "Good. Then let us stop wasting time with these existential conversations. Navigate this ship."

As I moved to the instrument panel, Muri swiped at his muzzle and chuckled. "It is interesting, Captain."

"What's interesting?"

"How the old hierarchies have been flattened."

Out the window the perforated cliffs of Seed Island appeared very far away.

4

The sun was setting by the time the rocky knob we'd informally christened Seed Island appeared through the heavy mist, sparkling with recently dispersed sulfate particles. The bears had moved the remaining crew into the hangar and split them up among the steel enclosures in which they themselves had lately been confined. Those who now walked the ship, with escorts, were Wagner, the head engine room engineer Cruz, young Messersmith, and myself.

As for me, I had not been left alone for a moment, so it was in Muri's presence that I spoke to Wagner and Cruz frankly about our dilemma. Cruz, ignorant of our contractual bind, felt that requesting assistance because livestock had escaped did not preclude future work at sea, especially if that future work did not involve livestock. Wagner, who had signed the same contact I had, of course refused to consider the idea of trying to call for help. He had a young family he wished to see again. Then Cruz—a genius with machines but not blessed with a great deal of common sense—pointed out that once help arrived and others saw the bears could speak, these problems would disappear. Neither Wagner nor I bothered to point out the obvious fact that the bears would immediately revert to the kind of biological behavior humans expected of them.

Muri said nothing during this discussion, but I knew he had absorbed every word. He and Latufa held hourly conferences in which they communicated in chuffing noises and occasional periods of silent gazing. In this way plans and designs had been coordinated. I marveled at the way the smaller Muri commanded the much larger Latufa's loyalty and obedience. I could not understand how Muri had established his dominance over such a creature. Despite Latufa's regal bearing, he was nothing more than a servant.

The seas were choppy now. We were still riding the Labrador Current, and there were spilling breakers visible on the other side of the island, so I tried to buy some time. Anchoring near the island was going to be difficult. However, Muri said the bears could now smell the seals and would not be made to wait. Wagner retrieved the assistant chief mate, a Russian we called Tsarskya, from his steel enclosure and accompanied him to the forestation to walk back the anchor. Tsarskya's eyes were just visible above his frost-spackled neck gaiter, and when I looked into them, I could read nothing. His brain might as well have been floating in a jar of formaldehyde for all it was engaged at the moment.

I moved to put the dock clutch into gear for him, but Latufa moved his body in front of mine. After gently nudging his old mother out of harm's way, he then lowered his head and with his shoulder pushed the dock clutch open. If my perceptions had been keener, if I'd not dismissed Tsarskya's demeanor as that of a traumatized man simply going through the motions, a man exhibiting only the nobility of the kidnapped, I might have anticipated his actions. But I too was stunned and had foolishly taken solace in those elements of ship-board protocol and routine that, despite all that had happened, were still in place, duties that included the walking back of a fourteen-ton galvanized steel anchor in a freshening wind.

Tsarskya stationed himself behind the anchor brake, and a group of bears gathered around the windlass gypsy curiously as it began to turn and feed out the chain, made of massive, two-foot-long iron links, into the cold depths. The chain picked up speed and Tsarskya controlled the anchor's descent by engaging the brake, which resulted in a mechanical aria of metal on metal that flattened the bears' ears and caused a few to retreat.

As the chain picked up speed, flakes of rust erupted from the spurling pipe. The gypsy began to squeal. To the inexperienced eye, this violence is unsettling, even terrifying, but the momentary chaos is routine in anchoring a large ship. The ritual unfolded unremark-ably, so I turned my attention to the horizon off starboard to look for ships. For this reason, I didn't notice that Tsarskya had stepped away from the brake wheel, which now spun so fast that no hand could rest on it without being shattered instantly. I realized, with horror, that instead of a controlled descent to the ocean floor, our anchor, and the brutal chain to which it was attached, was in freefall. The wind-lass shook and groaned; I had already seen four shots of chain speed past us, at ninety fathoms a shot. With the guillotine bar disengaged I knew there was little hope of arresting the chain.

Straining to be heard over the screaming windlass, I commanded Tsarskya to take cover. His eyes were fixed on my face. They were empty. He was not a man but a shell. Through the choking haze I could see jagged orange flames sprouting and receding from the wheel. I shouted to Muri to get the bears away from the windlass immediately, but it was too late. As the last shots flew out wildly, the entire apparatus began to wobble. I dove to the deck just before the final shot, with its savage links of pure steel, flew off the wheel and whipped around the fo'c'sle like a serpent's tail before disappearing forever into the depths of the Labrador Sea.

The quiet now was profound. I heard a broken whimper from the other side of the windlass. I could not tell if it was man or bear.

5

Death had been instant for the old female. She had been pulped by a four-hundred-pound link, her broken body thrown at least thirty yards down the deck. The bears approached the motionless mass of fur warily, drawing near but taking great care not to make contact with the corpse. Latufa, however, barreled down the deck, swinging his head side to side. He skidded to a stop just inches shy of the dead bear and a queer hissing noise issued from his mouth, causing the others to cringe. Then came a sepulchral roar that turned my blood cold. Instantly, the other bears retreated downwind, their ears flat, their eyes downcast. Near the crane, I saw Wagner, with the coward Tsarskya in his grip. Their bloodless faces made them seem only half there, spectral witnesses to a nightmare.

Muri, who had not left my side, startled me with a throaty, close-mouthed rumbling that rose in volume before terminating in a rusty chuff. He breathed heavily, his flanks rising and falling in half-second intervals, but he remained otherwise still. He repeated his call to Latufa several times before the bear swung his head around to regard his leader. As I watched, Muri slowly rose onto his hind legs and produced a sound I had not yet heard him make: a soft, maternal hum that gently rose in volume before fading, rising once more, and then disappearing into nothingness, like a lullaby. I hardly understood what I was hearing but I was gripped by that old desire for presence, not the never-ending absence we'd all grown used to, and was momentarily overcome.

Latufa, though, displayed no immediate response to Muri's song. For agonizing seconds that stretched into minutes, the two bears— one standing like a man, the other immobilized by something like grief—remained in this clinch, as still as fossils, and the implication as awful.

Then Latufa raised his head and from his coal-black lips emerged the most awful sound I've ever heard. It was as if the Lion of Judah had opened the Book and let loose the thunder of the apocalypse. Muri observed this—observed but did nothing more. Presently, Latufa began walking toward us, his head hanging, and the sound he now made can only be described as sobs. Muri dropped back to all fours. Fearful, I took a step back, pressed now against the hateful windlass.

As he drew close, Latufa's cries diminished into occasional whimpers. Muri lifted his head. Slowly, submissively, Latufa stretched his neck toward Muri until their leathery noses touched.

All around me, the bears raised their heads and sobbed.

6

"I have decided to kill the Russian."

"Surely you don't believe it was intentional."

"Intention is immaterial. His death will provide a warning to your men."

"Please don't. He has a family."

"So did my deputy. And anyway, it cannot be prevented."

I did not know what this meant, so I remained silent. Muri moved to the door and called down something to the deck. A young bear he called Nared approached the stairs. They exchanged some words, and after some time and as the ship rolled in the increasing swells, Nared reappeared with Tsarskya. The man was barely alive, a limp doll in the bear's mouth. Still alive, but only just. Nared dropped Tsarskya to the deck gently, allowing a group of curious cubs an opportunity to inspect the body. Eventually, however, Nared took the moaning Tsarskaya in his mouth again and headed starboard.

"No," Muri said quietly, almost to himself, "that will not do." His sudden roar sent me reeling. Nared froze and looked up toward the bridge. Muri barked twice and Nared immediately dropped my assistant chief mate onto the oil-slick deck. I had no time to look away before the younger bear ripped out Tsarskya's throat. I fell against Muri's flank, gripping his fur so tightly that he growled in protest. As Nared carried what was left of Tsarskya abaft, Muri turned back toward the bridge, beckoning me to follow. "There is no justice but in small portions. Keep faith with us or you shall follow him."

That night I slept fitfully. I had been unable to draw the Precession near enough to the raw coast of Seed Island without risking a disaster. The departed anchor rendered the option of a distant mooring impossible. I'd seen the hungriest bears hanging over the railing, as if preparing to dive into the sea.

When I woke, Muri was sitting on his haunches in the corner of my quarters. A plate containing a raw four-horn sculpin had been placed on the side table. The fish was a primordial demon, a deformed skeleton with blade-like fins and bulging gelatinous eyes. I turned away. "You must eat," Muri said.

"I cannot."

Muri turned to look out the porthole, wistful. "The scent of the seals is driving the bears mad; even Latufa tried to climb overboard this morning."

"We can do little without an anchor. The sooner you let me return the ship to the Labrador Current, the quicker we'll be back home," I said.

"Put your second in a Zodiac, then. I'll send him with two hunters. Let them bring the seals to us."

"Wagner must not be harmed."

Muri agreed, so I returned to the bridge, took the helm, and maneuvered the ship to within two hundred meters of the island. The sea was rough; if not for the fact that the icebreaker had a double hull, we might have been dashed to bits on the stony shards that ringed the island. It did not help matters that the majority of the bears had abandoned their posts and rushed aft in order to see the seals that were massed on the beach, almost indistinguishable from the slick gray stones that surrounded them. Alarmed at the encroaching ship and its odoriferous passengers, the male seals set up an ungodly racket and sparked a mass exodus, leaving the whelping females defenseless.

Muri and I watched as bears and men worked together to launch the Zodiac from the davit. I thought I caught Wagner's eye as he sat motionless in the stern next to Nared, his hand on the tiller; but when I waved to him, he did not respond. His eyes were fixed on the western edge of the island. It seemed as if he were being pulled backwards, away from me, away from the world.

Once the boat had been lowered to the water, we all watched it zig over the breakers, Wagner's serenity contrasted by the barely restrained panic of the young male Muri had assigned to accompany my second. Only Nared remained in total control. Wagner attempted to make a landing but drew back due to some hazard invisible to those of us on the deck.

The Zodiac attempted a landing three times, turning back all three times in order to find a more hospitable spot. The seals had of course retreated far up the shore by this time, repulsed by the sound of the inflatable's coughing engine and the scent of the bears. On Wagner's fourth attempt, the young male leapt into the sea, unable to restrain his hunger any longer, and paddled toward shore. This sent the boat nearly vertical, and Wagner only just managed to keep his grip on the tiller as the inflatable righted itself.

"Yes, that's okay," Muri murmured next to me.

"We must keep the ship away from shore or we will run aground."

"Then do so."

As dusk approached, the Zodiac disappeared round the eastern edge of the island. The bear who had paddled to shore had also vanished. The *Precession* moved closer and closer to shore without ever seeming to gain distance, a trick of the light, perhaps, or a trick of the mind. The setting sun coated the western cliffs of the island in a sherbet glaze. With silent Muri at my side, I walked onto the observation deck to watch the stars rise. Within ten minutes, the sky was salted with them.

It was then that we saw the ship.

7

A long-ago decommissioned Coast Guard cutter, the *Cloud Seeder* was registered out of Greenland. In the first hours after we'd left Iqaluit, I'd heard over the radio that the captain and his ten-man crew were making a last sealing run before the season ended. Of course, since Muri and Latufa had taken control of the ship, I'd had no access to radar or radio, but I was not entirely surprised to see the cutter rounding the western edge of Seed Island. I guessed the *Seeder*'s inability to raise anyone on the *Precession* by radio would raise suspicions. I was torn by two powerful desires: the prospect of rescue and the desire to pass the *Cloud Seeder* with no communication in order to appear in total control of my ship.

Muri understood these desires without hearing them spoken aloud, and at turns thoughtful and agitated he paced the Navigation Room. Below us, the bears had moved en masse from the starboard side of the deck, where they'd been watching the progress of the Zodiac, to the port, where the *Cloud Seeder* was coming into view. They sneezed and coughed, tossing their heads as if shaking off blows. Muri spoke harshly to them and they quieted down. Latufa lumbered up from the galley, and he and Muri conferred quietly. Soon I was drawn into the discussion.

"Latufa is in favor of moving on immediately," Muri said.

"But our men are still out there," I said.

Muri looked at me strangely. "Our men? Have you thrown your lot in with ours?"

"You know what I meant, Captain," I said.

I had been unable to catch this last word before it left my lips; I knew not where it had come from, only that it had felt entirely natural. Muri had no opportunity to respond, because Latufa pounded the deck with his heavy left paw.

"What does he say?" I asked.

"Like everyone else, he's hungry for seal, but he feels a rendezvous with this vessel is too risky."

"And you?"

"I do not think I will maintain control of the vessel if we navigate away from the whelping grounds. Mutiny is nothing to starving souls." He glanced over at the ship, still a couple of miles away. "You say it's a sealer?" I nodded. "Then perhaps it's best to let them come."

"They will come regardless. And they will know something's wrong."

Muri hesitated and I could see that he was working it out, his nimble brain picking up and dismissing options. Then, arrived at a decision, and with a quick glance at me, he spoke to Latufa. The large bear at first seemed disinclined to listen, his eyes continually darting toward the whelping grounds, but he soon grew calmer, so calm, in fact, that he smiled, revealing a thick yellow canine that still bore traces of blood.

It was a simple plan, and after explaining it to me, Muri dispatched Latufa to instruct the rest of the bears and men, though not before reinforcing the plan to me with threats of bodily harm and death. "If you so much as give a look that hints at past events or the present state, I will kill you instantly." But I felt this was said for Latufa's benefit alone. Muri knew where I stood. I had no interest in calling for help and sentencing myself to the same kind of exile known by the crew of the *Marigold*. How much worse would my banishment be, having lost the ship to mutiny engendered by my own cargo? There was something else, too, though I could not yet acknowledge it, let alone understand it.

However, I knew the other captain might not be so behaviorally plastic. When I shared this thought with Muri, he smiled. "He will not see."

"How could he not?"

"I suspect that, just like all men, he clings to tranquilizing thoughts about his species' power."

8

Captain Robin Holmes was a lean, quick man, with a nut-brown beard that concealed a gaunt and pale face. His eyes took in all aspects of the icebreaker and found much that met with his approval. He'd been aboard the *Kapitan Khlebnikov* two decades earlier, before it had been put in dry dock. It was a former class 3 icebreaker then, which had been converted into a Northwest Passage cruise ship after terminal ice-out had been declared. The *Precession*, Captain Holmes said approvingly, compared well. "We tried to raise you several times, you know," he said. "We only pulled round because you were silent. Your computers down?"

"Hit a dead zone as we approached this latitude."

"We haven't had trouble."

"Bad equipment on our end. Boss trying to do it on the cheap. Government."

This satisfied the captain, even pleased him. After some talk of the recent bombing of Russia's base in the Laptov Sea, though, I began to sweat. Though he displayed curiosity about all other aspects of the ship's operations, he had not made any sign that he'd noticed Muri, beyond a brief hesitation upon boarding the ship and a few poorly concealed glances in the bear's direction during our tour of the ship.

My captor had disguised himself as a tame bear—a kind of pet— and now followed me around ploddingly; his cringing affect unsettled me nearly as much as Holmes's refusal to acknowledge what, to his eyes, must surely be strange and dangerous. Thoughts needled me relentlessly: *Does he know? Has he already called it in? Will he attempt to gain control of the ship?*

The rest of the bears had, at Muri's command, returned to their enclosures, though they would not consent to being locked in. Most of my remaining crew—a mix of low-level maintenance techs and support staff, such as a cook and a custodian—had been locked into the enclosures with the bears, terrorized into catatonia, though no other crew member had been so much as scratched since Tsarskya's brutal death. Some of the men were now convinced that the lunacy specific to this route was contagious and that they'd caught it. It was the only comfortable explanation, and the weaker men clung to it by lapsing into total silence.

Only Cruz, the engine master, who remained ensconced in the engine room with Latufa; Messersmith, who had been tasked with scrubbing the deck and who without an ability to speak was no threat; and Wagner, who remained somewhere on Seed Island, were at some facsimile of liberty. This, then, was the version of normalcy we presented: appropriately restrained polar bears on an icebreaker headed for Antarctica—a vessel, a route, and an itinerary that passed for normal in the New Abnormal.

Finally, after we'd walked the bridge and the observation deck, Holmes pointed to Muri. "Got yourself a pet, then. That's something special." Muri twisted his cuneate head over his shoulder to look into my face. Holmes noted this and added: "You think that's wise?"

With difficulty I managed to say something about how the last Baffin Bay pod were nearly tame, thanks to total habitat loss and a forced reliance on humans for food post-Impact. Holmes nodded grimly. "I suppose they're all something close to tame now, eating garbage and bear chow." He raised his hand as if he were going to lay it on Muri's head. I felt the rumble of Muri's low growl against my hip. Holmes heard it too and slowly pulled his hand back. "Ever worry this one will rear up and tear you to bits?"

This time it was I who sought Muri's eyes; they were glassed over now, as if he'd bifurcated from his being and was watching over the scene from an invisible vantage point.

"I suppose I'd be a fool not to."

Holmes gazed admiringly at Muri. "Well, I'd be lying if I didn't tell you I'm jealous of what you've got here with this animal. Tell me, what's his price?"

To my great shock, Muri began licking my hand. Dark and supple, his tongue lapped at my trembling fingers. Suddenly I was desperate to tell Holmes everything: how we'd loaded them at Frobisher Bay; how they'd willingly gone into the enclosures like milking cows into a barn; how the zookeeper had marveled at this uncharacteristic pliancy and then fallen quiet and thoughtful; how I'd been woken up that morning and taken to the Zodiac deck and how a full minute elapsed between the time I observed the mutilated crewman lying in a pool of blood, surrounded by polar bears, to the time I fully understood I was not still asleep; how from that moment until now Muri had not left my side; how he spoke, the slight gargle in the back of the throat; how he knew things about the world we shared; and how he knew just how badly and how irrevocably we had hurt it.

"He's government property," I said quietly, "so of course I can't sell him."

"Can't you?"

"I must give this bear credit. Somehow he keeps the other bears calm, keeps them in check when they have sometimes been tempted to—"

Holmes began laughing. "'Tempted'? You speak of them like they're people."

I was quiet for so long that Holmes grew serious. "Everything okay?"

"We've got a provisions problem. The bears won't eat the chow. Never did eat the bear chow that was dropped and won't eat the chow now. The last seal-eaters, this pod. They're hungry now; I'm worried they're going to make trouble." Holmes returned only an uncomprehending stare. "Look, I'm on the line financially for each one lost on the voyage, and since they've refused to eat from the time we threw off the ropes in Iqaluit, I'm in trouble. That's why I'm here." Holmes still said nothing, so I added, "I've got three crew members ashore right now trying to take seals and I've lost my anchor. Have you any carcasses I can buy?"

Now a smile lifted the corners of his mouth, revealing tobacco-stained teeth. "Let me see them first. The bears. I want to see them."

"They are agitated."

"Good. More interesting that way."

I longed to look at Muri for approval but felt Holmes was watching closely for just such a signal. Cringing, I dropped my hand onto Muri's muzzle; he lifted it under my trembling fingers, and by this I knew it was okay to bring Captain Holmes down to the enclosures.

We both made much racket as we approached the hangar where the enclosures were located, to signal any bears that may have stepped out temporarily, and I heard the sound of gates closing hurriedly. As we approached the door, Muri let out a harsh, rasping roar. Holmes stopped dead, his face drained of color, and to my surprise I felt him gripping my arm.

"It is nothing," I said. "The bear senses we are close; he is speaking to his brothers."

"You are too familiar with them, Captain."

I chose to ignore this. Holmes had to be reassured. We needed his seal meat and he needed his life. Of course, he only knew the former to be true; the second was strictly philosophy for him at this point.

The hangar door scraped and squealed, metal against metal, as it rolled upwards. An indescribable wet heat enveloped us at once, carrying on it the scent of musk, excrement, and spoiled bear chow. The bears were huddled in family groups—several cubs tumbled on the floor of one of the enclosures. Another, sluggish and glassy-eyed, sat on its haunches and stared at the wall. To my dismay, the dead female had somehow been carried to the back of the enclosure closest to port and was now poorly hidden by several younger females who had apparently been guarding her corpse. Off to one side, three of my remaining crew members stood at attention. Aside from the fact that they were unarmed, they betrayed nothing unusual. Holmes, however, noticed the lack of firearms immediately.

"Why are the racks empty?"

"We do not require guns with this group. They are docile."

Holmes wrenched his hand off my arm. "Fool. There's no such thing as a docile bear." He surveyed the bears, his eyes slowly moving from left to right. "How far to Antarctica?"

"Weeks."

"And how many are expected to survive the trip?"

"I do not know. We are not told expected mortality rate, only that we are financially responsible for each one that dies."

Holmes began pacing; the bears followed him with their eyes. The razor's edge we walked seemed to have grown finer. Though he was not a bright man, Holmes, it seemed to me, felt he was being tricked in some way.

Muri's fur bristled against my leg, and I saw that he was focused on one of the crewmen standing immobile as a scarecrow next to one of the enclosures; he seemed to be trying to catch Holmes's eye. I maneuvered the captain of the *Cloud Seeder* back onto the deck. "You do not know us," I replied. "So how can you know what is strange here?"

Holmes looked back at the bears once more. "I have some carcasses. We only want the pelts, of course." He chewed on a blackened nail. "Let me talk to you without the animal. I cannot think for fear that he will sink his teeth into me."

"I assure you that is quite impossible. I've had golden retrievers more vicious than Muri."

Holmes's eyebrows went skyward. "You've given him a name, then."

"That is his name," I said before I could stop myself. I dropped my head and collected myself. "I mean, the zookeepers—the vets—they give them names. Helps them tell one from the next. Forgive me, Captain, but time is of the essence. May I buy that seal off you? The bears are angry."

Holmes's eyes narrowed. "Angry?" Muri stepped on my boot to let me know my slip had not gone unnoticed.

"*Restless* might be the better word," I said. A sharp glance from Muri and I hastily added, "Of course, it's not their fault. How can you make a bear understand that it won't be imprisoned in a steel enclosure forever, that before too much time passes they'll have all the penguin and seal they want?"

"Don't be a fool. You can't make them understand anything. They are beasts, not men." Holmes paused for a moment, thinking. "Tell you what—why don't you come aboard my ship. Have a drink, look over the seal meat, and my men will help you haul it over." At these words, my heart leapt; I was filled with some kind of hope. I cast a long look portside at the sealer, which held steady in the freshening wind, the portholes on its starboard side warm with lamp light. Muri shifted his weight from his left to his right, his left hip sinking, while the other rose, and looked up at me yet again.

Holmes noticed. "Maybe he wants a drink, too."

The longer I delayed my answer, the more impatient Holmes grew. "Come on, man."

The threat was, of course, implied in Muri's tongue running over the knuckles of my left hand, the steady rhythm of his lapping, but it was also overt in the easily recalled images of Tsarskya's terrible death, and the early hysterics of my crew members when the mutiny had first taken place. If I were to say yes to Holmes—and, by saying yes, essentially try to make my escape—Muri suddenly turning on me and mauling me to death would not have surprised Holmes; it would have been what he'd been expecting the moment he'd stepped foot on the *Precession* and saw me with Muri by my side.

So the nameless hope died in me as quickly as it had arisen, and I said, "I cannot go."

At this moment, Messermith hauled himself up from his knees, his scrub brush dripping with soapy water. I saw he was weeping. He walked toward Holmes, his gait unsteady, his mouth agape. He stumbled once, then hauled himself back to his feet. Next to me, Muri growled loudly. Holmes looked at the bear in alarm. "Stay where you are, son," he cried out to Messersmith.

I tried to keep my voice steady. "Messersmith, return to your station at once." It was too late; I could see from his eyes that he was lost. His clothes were darkened with blood—his blood, shed during the attack that took his tongue. Holmes made no sign that he understood the implication.

Messersmith gripped Holmes's arm and tried to speak. The sight of his desperate efforts was awful, but it was the sound that was unendurable. It cannot be described. Holmes stared, horror-struck, as

Messersmith opened and closed his empty mouth. The captain could not tell what Messermith tried to say, but I could. *"Take me with you."*

Muri looked up into my face. His eyes remained as impenetrable as ever, but water had pooled in them, turning them into tiny mirrors in which I saw myself reflected back.

Holmes shook off Messersmith so violently the young man reeled backwards. It was only by some miracle he kept his balance on the wet deck. Holmes began to say something, then stopped, his eyes traveling from Messersmith to Muri, then to me. Finally, he said, "What the hell is happening on this ship?"

Messersmith threw back his head and from his ruined mouth came an ungodly sound. With no backward glance, no hint of his intentions, beyond the visceral cry, he ran at the portside rail and, with an agility I'd hardly suspected over the days we'd been aboard the *Precession*, leapt over it and threw himself into the sea.

Holmes stood perfectly still, his slight bowleggedness exaggerated by the lack of movement. He gripped the starboard rail to steady himself. "I don't know what you boys have got going on this ship, but it looks like it's a problem." He reached into his jacket and pulled out his cell phone. "How about I just get a couple of my men over here to help you?"

He spoke slowly, addressing me as if I were a madman, as if it were I who was dangerous and not the clever bear by my side. I wanted to grip him by the throat and shake him, shake him until he understood that this was not the problem; this was the result of the problem. The problem was not men leaping overboard or even polar bears demanding to be repatriated to disappearing land. The problem was men. We were the problem. There was no dream from which to wake. We were the authors of the nightmare. Why couldn't he see that?

As I began to speak, Holmes let the hand holding the phone to his ear drop, and the phone clattered to the deck. He was focused on something off starboard. I followed his gaze. Visible through the cowl of mist wrapped round the island Nared and Wagner walked over the slick rocks of the beach, as easy and comfortable as a man and his dog. Behind them was a towering pile of dead seals.

"You—you took the bears ashore?" Holmes sputtered. "How the hell . . ." I approached the rail to see what had struck him dumb. Wagner had dropped his hand atop Nared's head as they walked.

Holmes whirled on me, his wind-ravaged face full of fear. "Good god," he said, "it's true."

After seeing that his exclamation raised no response from either me or Muri, Holmes again brought his phone to his ear.

Something compelled me now to place my own hand on Muri's head. The bony contours of his cranium felt natural under my fingers, almost comforting. Holmes looked on in horror. "Put the Device away," I said. "Let us handle this like men."

After a very long pause, during which his mind must have been percolating with all sorts of ideas and plans, he let the phone fall to his side. In a quiet, almost childlike voice, he mumbled something I could not understand. I asked him to repeat himself, but he only shook his head.

"He asked you if you were man or bear."

Holmes, shocked into a stupor by Muri's speech, did not move a muscle, not even when my false pet raised himself up to his full height, leaned forward, and made a series of noises that I'd never heard—a mix of chuffing and panting that sounded almost like a saw pulling against tree bark. The awful sound continued for what seemed like a very long time but that was probably only a matter of seconds.

Holmes pointed at Muri. "It speaks," he cried, his voice high-pitched and tremulous. "It speaks!" He stumbled backwards, colliding with a pallet of bear chow. His eyes grew wild. He ran to port and for a moment I thought he, like Messersmith, was going to vault over the side. Instead, he waved his arms above his head, palms out, arms crossing and recrossing with increasing desperation, trying to gain the attention of his crew. His cries dissolved into the wind. Night had truly fallen now, and our floodlights were of course not on. The *Cloud Seeder* was a glowing toy boat, with warmly lighted portholes but no men visible on deck.

Holmes turned around and faced us. As if moving through water, he again reached for his phone. Only it wasn't his phone he sought. It was a handgun that he'd clipped to his belt, until now unseen beneath his parka. Though his hands shook, Holmes was able to raise the weapon and train it on Muri's head.

I stepped between Muri and Holmes's gun and begged for the bear's life, knowing I was also begging for Holmes's. Stupefied, the captain turned the weapon on me, then back on Muri, then on me again, his confusion so great that his eyes filled with tears.

The ear-splitting wail of the engine turning over surprised us all. As if mutes in congress, we stared at each other, trying to read meaning in a fleeting grimace, a darted eye. Because of this racket, and partly because of his shock at hearing Muri speak, Holmes did not realize Latufa approached him from behind.

9

It was some time later that Muri and I stood side by side on the bridge, while Holmes lay insensible on a cot near the instrument panel. He no longer responded to our questions, sinking in and out of consciousness. He only raised his finger to his lip and smiled, displaying the bloody gaps where his teeth, until very recently, had been rooted.

Holmes would later be found at what was once thought to be a phantom island off the coast of Greenland called Fata Morgana by an Argentina-bound freighter, bloodied and insensible, in the bottom of a Zodiac. Holmes spoke to his rescuers of a cursed icebreaker piloted by Baffin Bay bears and ably assisted by men. Naturally, his story was dismissed as the ravings of a man at sea too long, his mind infected by the indigenous belief systems of his Inuit crew.

After Latufa had neutralized Holmes, Nared and Wagner returned from Seed Island with piles of seals and without the young male who'd disappeared once on shore and for whom we could not wait. As we pulled out of the cove, we passed close enough to the *Cloud Seeder* to see the brown, weathered faces of the crew who had gathered on the deck. Not a sound arose from those men as we passed, and when Muri hailed them they returned the greeting. Within an hour, we were traveling the Labrador Current again, heading back the way we'd come, heading home, where some or all of us would die rather sooner than we'd like, but at least on our own terms.

Frosted air enveloped us while the ship plied ice-greased waters. Next to me, Muri made contented sounds in the back of his throat. My thoughts had drifted to what would happen when the *Precession* reached Nunavut. We could likely avoid official detection if we hugged the lawless coast of the Nunavut Land Claims Agreement Area and deposited the bears on Hall Beach, but what then? Would we men not eventually return to shore and be forced to answer for our incomprehensible failure? A litany of psych exams, exit interviews, and pre-Banishment physicals would commence before we faced our contractual obligations. I lingered only briefly on these details. They seemed unimportant compared to the fate that awaited the bears, who, now that they understood the ship was continuing north, inexorably north, ringed the deck and lifted their noses into the wind. They knew they had returned to the soggy permafrost of Qikiqtaaluk, to naked cliffs wreathed in methane mists, to beaches dusted with translucent oyster shells.

"It was no dream, then," I said. "I am not mad."

Muri shifted his weight so that his right flank touched my body. "What is considered madness by men is oftentimes nothing more than comprehension. You understand. It is because you understand that you allowed these events to unfold." My sharp look was returned with a chuckle. "Yes, you allowed it to happen because you understood it is no mutiny. It is just. You are just. No other man alive can say this."

I felt a sob rise in my chest. It broke my next words into pieces. "Why did you board, then, if only to force a return?"

Muri sighed deeply and for the first time appeared tired. "It is nothing to us now. We are finished. Our brothers already South will be dead before the year is out. We will be dead in a month, but we will be home. Our time is over. We understand that. But there must be a witness. A witness who will see. You will tell of this."

"But I will not be believed," I cried. "They will call it madness."

"They may call it what they like, but you will tell what you've seen, and eventually they will come to understand that though we go first, their time nears too."

The *Precession* seemed to enter some kind of naturalistic ante-room then, a space where the ocean grew still and smooth. I saw Latufa at the bow, his proud head lifted into the headwind, the body of his mother at his side, secure in the oilcloth into which I'd sewn her. The frazil ice softly rolled away from the hull as we moved north along imaginary longitudes to an imaginary place.

HONEYMOONS IN TEMPORARY LOCATIONS

"Crushed and jolted amid the apocalyptic exodus, waiting for unscheduled trains that were bound for unknown destinations, walking through the stale stage-setting of abstract towns, living in a permanent twilight of physical exhaustion, we fled..."

—"THAT IN ALEPPO ONCE...," VLADIMIR NABOKOV

Well, A, I'm sitting in the front parlor of the Glensheen Guest House for Internally Displaced Persons of Means, finally in the Promised Land. Let this missive serve as confirmation that I've safely arrived in a Climate Impact Resettlement Zone. Spread the word to our mutual friends and nemeses that with patience, persistence, and a valid Environmental Migrant Residency Permit, they too can be successfully resettled in the bluffs of climate-stable Duluth, provided their net worth is high enough.

Cedar is here. I ran into him yesterday afternoon at the highest point of North 19th Avenue East, one of several 45-degree angles masquerading as city streets here. He had tucked his longboard under his arm and seemed to be debating the wisdom of hurtling toward the vertex and into two lanes of no-emission traffic. We decided this

34

would not be the best inauguration for a successfully resettled refugee. By the way, it was Cedar, bless his artisanal gin-loving heart, who gave me your contact info (my phone was destroyed during the exodus under circumstances I'll share with you directly). He wanted me to "gently" mention that you still owe him for that borrowed carbon credit from last year. Consider it gently mentioned.

I have a story for you. I should warn you that this story differs from the ones we swapped at that dirty bar on Vandam Street pre-Breach, gobbling stale Goldfish mix from wooden bowls and double-fisting vodka tonics on "Laid-Ease Night." Whenever I think of the Great Manhattan Seawall Breach, by the way, I can coax out a laugh by imagining how the Hudson must have washed through that nasty hole in the wall, turning our beloved fish-shaped crackers into swollen monsters, and setting them free to explore upstream. Swim, little fishies, swim!

But this isn't about the origin of your mysterious bruises or my late-night adventures in the bathrooms at Sapphic Sips. No, this is a tale of existential confusion, and I want you to caper down the road to oblivion with me.

I don't think you know that I ended up marrying that girl after you left New York. This was a couple weeks before Superstorm XY came roaring through the city. And although I do have our certificate of marriage in my possession, along with our resettlement papers, I now assert that I was never married. I will go one step further. I am not convinced my wife ever existed.

Now I know what you're thinking—this is just another one of my tiresome metaphysical parlor games—but I assure you I am in earnest. This is quantum physics, A. Superposition, specifically. Process decoherence. Schrödinger's pussy. Here's the proposition: my wife was a wave-particle duality in human form. I married the wave but somewhere along the way lost the particle, and therefore the wave as well.

I know. It is an extraordinary claim. I will provide you extraordinary evidence.

First, the girl: you remember her. She was the Chapstick lesbian circulating at Grant's Net Zero party, the one who gave the toast about the carbon neutrality of biomass and how Grant's achievement of personal net zero was a "proof positive" of continuing human ingenuity. You rather loudly, if I recall correctly, ridiculed her reckless use of air quotes around *proof positive* and subsequently retired to the balcony with Jeff Meredith to get stoned.

I wasn't immediately smitten. She referred to herself as a Rapid Adapter, a term she immediately shortened to "RA," and bored me with talk of investments that would "unlock the doors to staggering impact-immune profits." She bragged about her brother's heirloom chickens. When she worked "proof positive" into the conversation a second time, I was ready to walk.

But then Wren—who was there with Lennon, natch—trotted out that story about seeing a group of children in Prospect Park holding a funeral for a dead tree, and she cried. And when she cried, A, she looked so vulnerable and so lovely that the hard spiral structure that passes for my heart opened like a fire-roasted pinecone.

Still, I remained circumspect. I decided to accompany her to the IRT, mostly because I was feeling protective, and I don't know, but something she said when we were standing there under the rusted trestles ignited something (my own biomass, perhaps?). She made me laugh, and you know how that goes with me.

Anyway, it was the funny thing she said, or the fact that the first rolling blackout of the night had just started or that we were close enough to the waterline that I could hear the river lapping against the dikes on 96th Street, or the low-grade humming of the generators so reminiscent of my battery-operated girlfriend—it was any or all of these things that pushed me into the abyss of infatuation. The feeling was returned by half: I suppose that she felt aerosol dispersal management was a stable job sector and that my wagon was as good as any on which to hitch her pulsating death star. We were married within a fortnight.

As you already know, I had been making plans to follow your example and apply for a residency permit in one of the Non-Impact Regions. My bride mentioned she had family in Duluth but had lost their contact information—much as I did yours, in fact—when she dropped her phone into a composting toilet at the Ersatz Café. This was slightly inconvenient. As you know, your residential permit application is fast-tracked if you have family in the Non-Impact Zone to which you're traveling. But, as her parents had gone radio silent since joining an eco-village in Bellingham and could not be petitioned for the contact info, we simply beat on, nonsovereign citizens against civil servants, borne back ceaselessly into the heart of bureaucracy. One day she handed me a temporary tattoo of a radish. An address and number were scrawled on the back. The aunt's. My wife indicated, somewhat abashedly, that she'd discovered it in an old Altoids tin she kept in the back of her closet (along with a Lake Superior agate, an Allen key, and a punch card from a tarot card reader, all souvenirs, she said, from a childhood visit to the aunt).

We called the number in the listing, but no one picked up. Our messages grew increasingly dramatic, I confess. These also went unreturned. Meanwhile, we waited for our papers.

Our hand was forced by the storm surge, and we were rounded up, along with the others on our block, and transported to the Migrant Transport Center up at the Cloisters. We were told to wait there for "unscheduled buses" that would take us to "temporary locations." I was too exhausted to ask how a location could be temporary, though now I've come to consider this question hopelessly naive.

We slept on cots in the Unicorn Tapestries Room, where, it seemed, they'd installed all the gay couples "out of abundant concern for our own comfort and safety." Three days we spent here, waiting for buses, for papers, for any indication of where we were headed, and in the meantime becoming very knowledgeable about the use of wool warp and gilt weft in medieval South Netherlandish tapestries. All we knew was that massive swathes of Manhattan were being evacuated and that each migrant would receive a resettlement notice eventually, but probably not until we had arrived at one of those mystical "temporary locations."

Those wise folk who left New York earlier, and of their own volition, like you, A, had a say in the matter of where they resettled. Us stragglers were at the mercy of the green *politburo*. This experience, incidentally, was the extent of our honeymoon. As we were sleeping on separate cots, I was only able to cop a couple feels by reaching across the cold marble floor before a security guard approached with a scowl and a poorly concealed hard-on.

Eventually, though, we made it to Chicago, the environmental migrant's Grand Central. She bore the whole adventure with a kind of dreamy optimism, saying little, but holding my hand all the way from the Pennsylvania Turnpike to the Indiana toll roads. Not even the roadside signs announcing SOLASTALGIA IS A STALINIST HOAX and MIGRANT SCUM KEEP DRIVING punctured our connubial contentment.

We were a couple miles past Gary, the ZEBS bus (Zero Emission Bus System) idling in a miles-long jam headed into Chicago, when she disappeared to visit the on-board bathroom. When she returned to her seat, her entire demeanor had changed. Her words were frost-flecked, her face impassive. She asked to exchange seats with me so she could be next to the window. Once reseated, she turned her back to me. Momentarily, she began to sob. "How could we have left him behind? The poor child. He'll never know why we didn't come back."

Her sorrow was immense; her face was wet with tears. Of course, we had no child. When I gently pointed this out, she nodded. "I know. I know. But what if we'd adopted that child?" I inquired about this child of whom I knew nothing. "The one from the National Alliance for the Resettlement of Gun Orphans. NARGO? Can you imagine? He'd be pacing the apartment, crying for us, wondering why we'd abandoned him. I can't bear to think about it."

She turned back to the window to look at the endless line of hydrogen-fuel-cell vehicles glinting in the sun. It wasn't worthwhile, I felt, to mention that we had never discussed NARGO, much less considered adoption. At the time I chalked up this strange exchange to exhaustion and displacement-induced anxiety.

We arrived at Union Station, where we spent several hours in several different lines, making our case for a temporary residency permit for Duluth. As a Non-Impact Zone, Minnesota is in high demand among migrants from the East Coast cities, for obvious reasons. (You know what happened to Wren and Lennon when they ended up in

Green Bay.) Thanks to my wife's mysterious Duluth aunt, we were given approval papers and directed toward a St. Paul–bound train. We had to make our way through a boisterous mob in possession of lots of handmade signs and a single tooth (ha), and one of our cohort got into a shoving match with a guy who called him a "taco jockey" (the taco jockey was in fact a Syrian-born professor of antiquities at NYU).

The ride was unremarkable for the first two hours. The towns along the route were all official environmental migrant resettlement sites, taking advantage of that generous federal subsidy about which you argued with me so vehemently at the Mets game we attended last summer.

Eventually, the train pulled into a Wisconsin town called Tomah. We'd run out of food by this point, so I disembarked alone in search of provisions (she was still too distraught about the nonexistent orphan to leave her seat). I was gone a total of six minutes, which was apparently two minutes too long, because when I returned to the platform with a fistful of energy bars, the train was gone.

At the ticket office, where I sought counsel, the agent was instantly agitated. He sprang up from his swivel chair and jabbed a finger at me. "You had no right to get off!" Ecoauthoritarianism at its finest. I didn't linger.

I wandered over to the train tracks to plan my next move. But as I looked down the line toward St. Paul—for what purpose, I cannot say—my phone made its escape from the unzipped right-breast pocket of my Carhartt utility vest (one of *Glamour*'s "Must-Have Pieces for Evacuation Journeys"). It landed with a sickening splash in a pool of hydraulic fluid between the wall and the third rail. I briefly considered leaping down to retrieve it but decided I was unwilling to risk death, particularly since the last words I'd hear before impact would undoubtedly be, "You had no right to jump off!"

Thus began my bureaucratic nightmare. I won't bore you with the minutia of my aggravations, but suffice it to say that since neither she nor I now had a phone, we had no way to communicate. I did what I thought best at the time, which was to board the next train that came through and disembark at the next resettlement stop (the aptly named La Crosse, Wisconsin). Surely, she would have gotten off at the first opportunity once she realized I had been stranded. However, she wasn't at La Crosse. I imagined her, frantic with nervous energy, scrambling to the other side of the tracks to take the train back to Tomah, hoping to find me. What if she were there now, suffering the admonishments of the ticket agent?

So I returned to Tomah. You can probably guess that she wasn't there. Now I was caught in a loop. As I munched on one of the energy bars I'd procured for her, I thought about the gun orphan. Was he real and I'd simply forgotten? Or, more ominous, was he imaginary, and she just thought he was real?

This would've been a fun brainteaser for us in better times, but as I sat there on a bench in the empty Tomah train station, I entertained for the first time that my wife did not in fact exist, and that I was in pursuit of an entity that was no more real than the orphan she mourned. I dismissed the thought as the ravings of an exhausted mind.

I arrived in St. Paul the next day and took a bus across the Mississippi to Minneapolis, where the New York migrants had gathered in a neighborhood called Longfellow—a place crisscrossed by old rail lines and rehabbed grain elevators. A uniformed resettlement officer gave me directions to the hostel where the rest of the New York migrants had been relegated, and I checked in—asking, of course, after my wife. She had not been heard from, so I made my way to the Minneapolis resettlement office, hoping for better luck. There, I produced papers, our wedding certificate, and my wife's own notice of resettlement, which I'd kept nestled next to mine in the left thigh pocket of my Dickies.

Bureaucracy having received its portion, I was told again that no one had seen her. I contacted the police, who were of no help whatsoever. One officer, upon inspecting our marriage certificate, claimed it was invalid because the notary's seal hadn't completely perforated the paper. Still, he took down my information and claimed that he'd look for my "lady-wife."

That night, I ate dinner at the neighborhood café where my fellow displaced New Yorkers gathered to watch CNN's coverage of Superstorm XY, and to trade information about the friendliest enclaves for refugees. I learned that the Syrian professor had been taken into custody earlier that evening and was being questioned at the Hennepin County Courthouse for alleged ties to a Mexican carbon-trading scheme. I did not, however, learn anything about my wife. I slept.

The next day I purchased a new phone and used it to post a Missed Connections ad on Craigslist, where it was immediately lost in a blizzard of other *Looking for . . .* entreaties. I noticed I didn't miss her, though this didn't strike me as odd at the time. I just wanted to know where she was. *If* she was. I provided my new number to the appropriate authorities and checked into my assigned hostel, where I locked my belongings in a cage box and eventually fell asleep after my lower bunkmate completed his onanistic pursuits.

After breakfast the next morning, I made my usual rounds. Still no word—not from the authorities, not from the other migrants loitering on the streets of Longfellow waiting for papers and instructions and vouchers and carnets, not from the anonymous hordes perusing Craigslist. I thought about reaching out to our New York coterie, in case she had somehow made her way back across the checkpoints, but, strangely, I could think of no one to ask. It was then I realized my wife and I had no mutual friends. There was no one, besides faceless mandarins, of whom I could inquire after her whereabouts.

I wandered around Longfellow, waiting for word. Naturally, I made my way to the nearest highway underpass to examine local graffiti: you will remember my grad school thesis "Deviance Gracility and Non-Normative Claim Staking on Transportation Infrastructure." Despite the state's reputation for being "nice," Minnesota's graffiti game was far from passive-aggressive: *If climate were a bank, it would have been saved*, one graffito read. Another said, *from this moment despair ends and tactics begin*. I saw *Climafeel is a weapon of mass destruction* and *We deserve everything bad that happens to us* and *The bears spoke in order to tell us that we broke the world*. Fascinating stuff.

Minnesota was temperate in November. After finishing off the last of the hated protein bars that had been the cause of my current difficulties ("Migrant's Friend Protein Solution, Salted Caramel"),

I made my way over to Minnehaha Park where I spent the afternoon marveling at the orange-gold and garnet leaves lifting lightly in what could pass as a harvest wind. Though the falls had stopped laughing two years earlier, the rocky precipice over which the waters used to cascade was still something to behold. Even as things vanish around us their absence reveals a different kind of beauty.

I remained in the park for hours, until the gloaming urged passersby to return to the well-lighted streets of Longfellow. Soon, the park was empty, though I suspected hidden figures bedding down for the night in unseen places all around me. My phone had been silent all day. I was desperate to find her, but I still did not miss her. I could not understand why. Perhaps it is difficult to miss people who may not exist.

I thought about standing up, but my limbs were lead. I could not make myself move. I suspect that had anyone passed by at that moment I could easily have been mistaken for one of those metal sculptures sometimes affixed to city benches. But instead of encountering a bronze-cast old man in a trilby with an arm thrown carelessly over the back of the bench, my imaginary flaneur would instead find a thirtysomething woman in sensible footwear sitting forward, elbows on knees, staring at a phone that offered her all the bad news she could stomach but nothing of the good.

I had just willed myself to stand up when a cloud of gray feathers landed on a nearby picnic table. It took a moment before the vibrating plumage became distinguishable as two owls. One large, one small. The larger owl stretched its wings. The smaller one was obviously sick—its eyes were half-closed, its feathers a mess. Its wings hung limply. It made a small, sad sound.

As if called forth by the owl's sob, or by my own imagination, an elderly man appeared, wielding a walking stick. He swung it toward the owls, causing them to fly into a defoliated oak nearby.

"Leave them alone!" I was surprised at the sound of my voice. I sounded like an affronted child. I leapt up from the bench and walked over to where the man stood shielding his eyes with a gnarled hand as he peered into the shadows. I snatched the stick from his grasp, fighting the urge to break it over my thigh. Instead I shook it at him. "What is wrong with you?"

The man's gray-blue eyes were lucid. He was untroubled by my outburst. "You are lucky you do not hear them. They ask some of us to take on their pain," he said. "And I have. I have carried it. But I can't do it anymore. Any longer and it will kill me. Let them find someone else."

He took his walking stick back and raised it skyward. "Pray for the truth of this world to be revealed, and then look for good and productive ways to satisfy your pain."

He limped away into the darkest part of the park. In the tree, the owls watched me as if they were weighing my soul.

Shaken, I returned to my room at the hostel, where there was a message from a police officer asking me to meet him at the YMCA downtown. The place was as seedy as you'd expect—an old SRO of the sort that used to haunt every city block above 96th Street, but that, in Minneapolis, is termed "transitional housing." I met the officer in the lobby, and he told me, "Your lady-wife has been found."

I followed him up the back stairs to a room where he burst in on a couple in bed. Needless to say, the woman in question was unknown to me. She and her bedmate, a doughy man covered in nautical tattoos, gazed back at us serenely, as if such intrusions happened frequently. The officer kept trying to get the poor woman to confess that she was my wife, until she finally said—and you'll appreciate the echo of Wren and Lennon's one-woman show in this—"I don't go in for that girl-and-girl stuff, Officer."

I walked back to Longfellow alone, and it was at the tail end of this solitary amble that I spotted her at the end of a long line of people queued up at the back of a Red Cross truck dispensing MREs and blankets. When I called her name, she turned her head but stood rooted to the ground. I sprinted over and took her in my arms. Her first words to me were, "I hope these meals are vegan."

A, she told me a tale that night, one so banal that I hesitate to share it with you. But because it speaks to this question of nonexistence, I might as well tell you that after the train took off without me that day at Tomah, she did in fact disembark at the La Crosse station. Instead of crossing the tracks and taking the eastbound train back to Tomah to find me, she went to the Commissariat (the La Crosse Department of Environmental Migrant Management). They were no help, and as she had no papers with which to board the next St. Paul–bound train (I had all of our papers, remember), she fell in with a group of North Carolina refugees in a similar bind. Together, they spent the night in an abandoned microbrewery on the outskirts of town, and the next morning she was able to borrow a carbon credit from one of the migrants—Cedar will probably try to claim that one, too—and use it to get on a ZEBS bus to Minneapolis. Her friendly seatmate advised her to go directly to Longfellow, where the New York migrants gathered. At the café, she had heard from some patrons that a rugged woman of average looks had been looking for her. She said she figured I'd find her and so did nothing to find me, convinced that two people looking for each other will never meet.

I accepted this story. After three days of exhaustion, existential angst, and travel-induced constipation, I lacked the strength required to interrogate my wife. We took advantage of the near-empty hostel to engage in coital activities. It was in the middle of these marital affections, as her strong thighs flanked my head, that she became unresponsive. I ceased my efforts, to see what the matter was. She gazed down at me impassively. "I lied to you," she said. "Before. When I told you about the brewery and the people from North Carolina. I never got off at La Crosse. I met a man on the train. He was a salesman."

Over the next few hours, as we lay together in a top bunk and the other migrants straggled in, I got the story out of her crumb by crumb. She revised continually. What to believe? The first time they had sex, she said, was in the luggage compartment near the front of the train, and she'd been "too tired to care." The second time, during the Hudson stop, they met in the same place because she'd decided that I'd deliberately left her at Tomah and had no intention of returning. I probed, A. I was the Jacques Cousteau of sexual details—nothing was too insignificant to escape my notice. Had he bent her over the crates of ready-to-eat meals bound for the Twin Cities resettlement office, or had she sat upon the crates herself, opened her legs, and let him thrust against the cases of field rations? Was he a breast-cupper or a nipple-pincher? Was he a grunter? I half-hoped he was, because rhythmic ape-like grunting has always struck me as one important point of divergence between the straight man and the self-respecting gay woman. But even this she wouldn't confirm, telling me, "I wasn't listening."

Because of our paperwork problem, this back-and-forth between us went on for what seemed an eternity. The nonresidency permits were being held up for reasons that changed every time I inquired. We were buried by paperwork, benumbed by documentation. I was up all night filling out online forms I'd already submitted several times, beset by a caravan of rainbow wheels of death. The images of her failed flood insurance salesman (this was a detail she let slip) and his grunting lust blended seamlessly into the chiaroscuro of government documents and bored regional officials unwilling to even look up our permit status.

It all came to a head one day when we'd left the hostel to make our daily check of our permit status. We decided to walk through Minnehaha Park, where I'd spent those first days waiting. I tried to tell her about the owls, about the old man and his walking stick and his epigrammatic nonsense, but as I tried to tell her—*they ask some of us to take on their pain*—I was suddenly afraid it was I who now spoke of an illusion, an ignis fatuus, an orphan boy who didn't exist. She said nothing as I wept, as silent as a broken sump pump.

After I'd regained some semblance of control, she took my hand between hers and denied the whole thing had ever happened. There had been no salesman.

I had no idea how much time lay before us, whether our permits would be ready within days, weeks, or even months. (The self-abuser in the bunk below ours had been waiting for a permit for an Iron Range relocation since last spring.) Because our fates were intertwined by paperwork, we remained together.

I made the daily forays to the relocation office to check on our permits. She monitored the situation online. It was like living full-time with a failed blind date. But it was worse than that. We were estranged. This, coupled with the emotional morass of displacement, created a feeling of complete isolation. The first days of silence that passed during this contest between us were brutal and wintry. They formed a neat stitch of time that didn't quite close the wound. A, your cynical, worm-eaten heart will scoff at this, but though I didn't miss her when she was gone, and though I was not sure she was entirely well, I loved her desperately.

Now I come to the moment when I came to believe she had never existed. Our permits were in. I left to retrieve them and to secure our seats on the Duluth-bound train. I didn't know how we were going to move past all this, but for the first time in two weeks I felt sanguine.

However, when I returned to the hostel, she was gone. Her hemp-fiber purse, her two dresses, her duck boots, the Altoids tin—everything she'd brought to Minnesota had disappeared along with her. I looked for her everywhere, of course, and walked the paces. I asked everyone at the hostel if they had seen her. Not only would none of them speak to me, they also seemed angry and disapproving. I was flummoxed by their unwillingness to help.

Finally, one of them deigned to speak to me, an elderly woman named Kate who was wearing purple legwarmers despite the late autumn heat. "You are a terrible person for what you've done," she scolded me, jabbing her arthritic finger in my face. "I've never heard of such behavior."

It turns out, A, I'm a boor. Turns out—again, echoes of Wren and Lennon, who if they catch wind of this misadventure will co-opt it entirely—that my wife had hooked up with a prepper from Mankato named Rosie (natch) who had promised her a luxury underground bunker, a migration-free life, and plenty of hot meals. (It is with no satisfaction that I remind you that the prepper plutocracy I'd loudly predicted those first months post-Impact has in fact been established.) They'd connected online before we left New York.

I also learned that during those hours when I was out at the relocation office, supplicating and petitioning, my beautiful wife was holding the talking stick at the café and telling tales of my cruel refusal to grant her a divorce in order that she might fly away with Prepper

Rosie. Apparently, I had not responded well to this news. I'd threatened murder-suicide. I'd denounced her love affair and said I'd rather see us both dead than travel to Duluth alone. I'd made inquiries at hardware stores about rat poison.

The details my elderly scold shared were so pointillist in nature that I was unsurprised when, as our conversation came to a close, she gripped my wrist and made me swear not to buy a gun and take off after the lovebirds (who, she told me, were already ensconced in a bunker beneath the terminal moraine of Blue Earth County). When I asked Kate if she'd ever seen Rosie the prepper queen, she confessed she hadn't, but had been shown a blurry cell phone picture (where'd my wife get a new cell phone?) and declared Rosie "rough but handsome."

By this time, Kate had ceased pointing at me with her twisted index finger, having calmed down considerably. But just before I left, she rapped on the side of the bunk three times with her bony knuckles and said, "One thing I won't forget, and will never forgive you for, is how you abandoned that poor little orphan."

I spent the days remaining before my scheduled departure trying to parse out whether the insurance salesman was the prepper queen, whether it was the other way around, or, more horrifying, if I'd invented all of them, including my wife. I gave up looking for her at this point—searching the streets of Longfellow was pointless, and asking after her at the café would yield nothing, not now that the story of my apparent cruelty had spread throughout the New York diaspora. I boarded the train to Duluth alone.

I sat across from that Syrian professor who'd been taken in for questioning when we arrived in Minneapolis. He inquired after my wife, wondering if she had remained in the sleeping car because she gets motion sickness, as his wife did. When I told him I traveled alone, he simply stared at me. "Forgive me," he finally said. "Perhaps I'm not thinking of the right woman, but I believe I saw your wife this morning, walking along East 26th Street. She told me you were on your way to meet her with your relocation permits, which had just come in. She looked happy."

And this, A, is the atomic nucleus around which this entire story revolves. This is the moment I accepted that she was nothing more than a thought. And lest you think this wishful thinking, let me add that once I arrived in Duluth, and just before I saw Cedar teetering atop West 5th Street on his longboard for the first time, I went to the address she'd given me, where her aunt maintained a home, the basis on which we received our relocation permits. It was a bike shop. The proprietor had never heard of anyone with my wife's family name.

This, my old friend, is where the story ends (the whimper implied). I am alone now, waiting for the State of Minnesota to issue my work authorization paperwork, with time to think about what Rosie the Prepper and a faceless flood insurance salesman gave my wife that I couldn't. Maybe it's that everything I wanted to give her had already been taken from me. I can just hear you scoffing, but what was taken from me was also taken from you.

Do you remember when we were children, A? I know you don't like to talk about it, but do you? Do you remember when we were the ones performing funerals for trees and how we agreed we would never step on ants because they have a heart—"a little one," you used to say. Of course, the adults beat that compassion out of us, telling us we would not survive in this world if we cared for little hearts. So we forgot that paper was made from the bodies of trees, that new homes were built from their bones and guts, that birds knew things, and that the Earth had a soul. But that wasn't enough, because then they revised their histories and inscribed over their shame so we wouldn't know what they'd done. Finally, they demanded that we let go of the world. It was natural to let go, they said. *Look at the trees that stop fighting infestation and begin their philanthropy. See how the leaves stop eating light when the weather grows cold, how the worms cure to death on the pavement after the rain.* They turned the letting go into an ethic.

I won't let go this time, A, because woman or ghost, wave or particle, I loved her. I loved her duck boots and her dresses. Her tears for imaginary orphans. Her *proof positive* and the feel of her hand in mine. I loved her because she was there and because she was not there.

You'll say I've grown tiresome. I can see you laughing about this with Wren and Lennon. You never had any patience for talk of love. After all, you consider it nothing more than automimicry, a false head on a butterfly's wing. You spoiled on love when you learned what they did to the world they told us they loved. You let go of it, along with everything else, denied it was real, called it a firefly taken for a star. I should've done the same. Perhaps if I had done so earlier, none of this would have happened. But I can't let go of love, A. I'm a small, pathetic creature, and to small creatures living in the dark, a firefly gives off as much light as a star.

DOCUMENTS (RECOVERED)

POST-IMPACT CRAIGSLIST ADS

HOT VAN TIME—M4W (FAR ROCKAWAY, NEW YORK)

Body: *Fit* **Height:** *6'3"* **Carbon Status:** *in compliance*
I lost my Civic in the most recent massive flooding event so I opted for
a van this time. No back seats, tinted windows. If you have a fantasy
I can help with, let me know. Can travel.

DAMSEL IN DISTRESS?—M4W
(GREENWICH, CONNECTICUT)

Body: *Lots to Love* **Height:** *5'7"* **Carbon Status:** *in compliance*
Did Superstorm XY send you packing? Looking for some help? Do
you have a talent you can share? I live in a Non-Impact Zone and have
a spare Environmental Migrant Residency Permit to share with the
right lady. Must be from an Impacted Community. Prefer BBWs just
a few pounds shy of the Federal Overconsumption Tax threshold.

BABE LOOKING FOR JESUS AT TINDERBOX LOUNGE ON
HALLOWEEN—M4W (ST. AUGUSTINE, FLORIDA)

Body: *Athletic* **Height:** *6'6"* **Carbon Status:** *Under Review*
I was dressed as a studly FEMA Director Jesus at Tinderbox last night
and I kept seeing posts from some girl looking for "Jesus" to meet

her in the third stall of the bathroom. I was on my way to the johns to find you when the evacuation order came in. Your pics showed a girl dressed up as a Displaced Person of Middle Eastern Descent. Despite your racist costume, I was cosplaying Our Lord and Savior, so I forgive you and would love to bestow some heavenly graces onto thou. Hit me up if you're the girl I'm talking about. Hopefully you were hot. It was hard to tell with that hijab you had on. Willing to throw in a few Federal Fuel Stamps if you end up being at least a seven.

FLOOD RELIEF HOTTIE—M4M
(CHARLESTON, SOUTH CAROLINA)

Body: *Dad-Bod*   **Height:** *5'10"*   **Carbon Status:** *Suspended*
You: National Guardsman working flood relief during most recent storm surge event. Me: stranded homeowner who should've known better than to buy near the floodplain. You were in the rescue bucket when the helicopter arrived, told me to leave my "man-purse" behind (it's an attaché, actually). Although it was too loud for conversation, I thought I sensed a spark. If you see this, tell me the name of the street my house used to be on.

RIDE WANTED: HEADED NORTH
(SANTA MONICA, CALIFORNIA)

This is a long shot, but putting this out there just in case. Like everyone else, I'm looking for a ride out of California, basically ASAP, until the fires die down. I'm not particular about where I'm dropped off, just ask that it be within the Federal Designated Safe Zone, preferably the Upper Mississippi River Basin. I am very good at gas jugging. Only luggage is my surfboard. Can help load or unload on both ends. Currently located at the Evacuation Gathering Point on the Pier. I'm the one with the Spongebob Squarepants shortboard.

ROOM FOR RENT: IMPACT-FREE HOME
(APPLETON, WISCONSIN)

If you're looking for a handout, you can just stop reading right now. This ad is for EMPLOYED people only with NO Excessive Carbon Usage violations that will result in a midnight visit from the FEDS. If you pass that test, read on: we're seeking a roommate for a laid-back house. Not many rules here, but there are two and they are VERY IMPORTANT: Number 1. No black market fuel in the house of any kind. We've been busted before, and it wasn't pretty. Save us all some grief and get your fuel legally. Sure, it's hard, but people do it every day. Number 2. No violence of any kind, not even a raised voice. There have been a couple of minor issues but we have worked them out MATURELY. If you're still holding on to some existential anger about runaway climate change, move on. We're okay with Environmental Migrants AS LONG AS YOU ARE EMPLOYED. Another important thing is paying your rent on time. Late payments will NOT be tolerated, and I don't want to hear any sob stories about long lines at the Bartered Goods Cash Conversion office. This is a cash-only thing—no produce or bulk foodstuffs will be accepted. C-A-S-H. My house is the only one on the block with Christmas lights (I hoard my carbon credits all year for this, in case you're judging). Also, liking the movie *Heaven Is for Real* is a good sign.

JOBS AVAILABLE: SICK OF BEING EVACUATED?
(ANYWHERE)

Has your local Evacuation Gathering Point become like a second home? Are you tired of waiting floods out on your roof? Why not experience emergency evacuations from the other side: apply to become a member of the National Disaster Resilience Corps (NDRC). We are currently seeking highly motivated people who want to make a difference in the community for opportunities in the following project areas:

Ironic Hedonist Dispersal Project

Prepper Engagement Initiative (exceptional people skills a must)

Perpetual Evacuation Management

Vertical Farm Inspections Team, Soil-Free Division

NDRC corpsmen and women receive generous increases in Federal Fuel Rations for each six months of uninterrupted employment, as well as housing in Safe Zones for themselves and their family members. Monthly allotments of High Demand Foodstuffs and Endangered Grains are based on performance reviews.

NOTE: This is a branch of the U.S. military and enlistment is required.

SUPPORT GROUP FOR RECENTLY DISPLACED MILLIONAIRES (NEWPORT BEACH, CALIFORNIA)

Are you one of the hundreds of high net worth Newport Beach homeowners whose beachfront properties were recently deemed uninhabitable under the Federal Post-Climate Impact Human Resettlement Act? Are you having a hard time adjusting to living full-time in your second or even third home? These changes can be difficult to handle. We invite you to share your stories of displacement in a safe environment with people facing the same struggles as you. In this group we will talk about how we face our changes in circumstance, examine our anger and helplessness in the midst of unexpected domestic downsizing, speak openly about forced interaction in mixed-income society, and share strategies for coping with the loss of square footage and ocean views. This is not a drop-in group. Pre-registration is necessary, along with a copy of your most recent tax return.

RANTS AND RAVES: IMMIGRANT TIDE (DES MOINES, IOWA)

What exactly is wrong with Midwesterners? You want to destroy yourselves all because you think this country is a "melting pot"? Stand up like men to the environmental migrant invasion. We don't need Texans in Iowa.

IMPACT CRUISES' BROCHURE TEXT

"Endangered Cities 7-Day Free-Sail Cruise"

The unexpected rapidity with which our country has been affected by climate change impact has left many seasoned travelers reeling, soaked with regret over missed opportunities to explore our domestic jewels now threatened by rising sea levels. Others find themselves uncertain about the global regulations on the cruise industry and the mandated shift to carbon-neutral, small-ship, free-sail cruising.

Impact Cruises offers the thoughtful traveler an unparalleled experience through its Endangered Cities 7-Day Free-Sail Cruise, fashioning a cruise experience for our treasured guests that taps into their passion for the history, culture, and wonders of the pre-Impact world. From Boston's vanished Back Bay neighborhood and the floating artificial islands of Miami to the last remaining dry-footed building in Savannah, Impact Cruises aims to give its guests a taste of the past, the present, and the future.

Immersion is a core principle of the Impact Cruises philosophy, and where possible we invite our guests to come "ashore" to experience the charms of cities like New Orleans, Miami, and Savannah.* Our experienced dinghy captains will lead small groups around cherished

---

* Not all ports of call are available for traditional disembarkation due to sea level rise and individual cities' State of Submersion (SOS).

landmarks, such as the spire of St. Louis Cathedral in Jackson Square and Boston's last remaining island neighborhood, Beacon Hill. In Miami, unparalleled scuba experiences await the avid diver, including excursions into the submerged charms of South Beach.[†]

These cities will officially become Restricted Impact Territorial Zones (RITZ) in a few years. Don't rob yourself, or your family, of the opportunity to take one last look at our vanished coastal cities, while enjoying the luxurious appointments you've come to expect from Impact Cruises.

Cities include:

Boston

Baltimore

Norfolk

Charleston, South Carolina

Savannah

Jacksonville (expires next year due to federally mandated
    transition to Complete Municipal Submersion [CMS])

Miami

New Orleans

TERMS AND CONDITIONS

Fares are quoted in U.S. carbon credits and are based on double occupancy. Fares do not include prepaid charges, optional facilities and service fees, or global carbon tax apportionments. Also not included are shore "excursions," gratuities, federal geoengineering surcharge, state and federal Engineered Iceberg Deployment fees, and Sulfate Particle Dispersal duty. Sea level fluctuations may impact the order in which cities are visited, or whether they are visited at all. Sulfate Particulate Showers cannot be forecast in advance and will affect the timing of arrivals and departures. The timing of International Cloud Brightening Drone Missions are not disclosed to the public in advance and will affect levels of sunlight, in some cases for weeks.

[†] Requires additional Release of Liability form.

UNICORN INVESTMENTS NEWSLETTER

Subscription Confirmation E-mail

From: Jack Marcelo, Chief Imagination Officer,
Unicorn Investments, Inc.

To: Jeffrey Meredith [jmeredith_812321@yahoo.com]

Subject: Unicorn Investments: PLEASE CONFIRM SUBSCRIPTION

Dear Jeff,

Thank you for subscribing to Unicorn Investments' twice-daily news-letter: you have taken the first step toward making savvy investment decisions during this time of upheaval. As you know, times are "hot" for getting rich in a climate-challenged world. The question is: can you adapt, and if so, how quickly? RAs (Rapid Adapters) are in an enviable position when it comes to investments. Subscribing to this newsletter proves you are an RA or at least RA-curious.

Jeff, per federal law, you must confirm your subscription. Please click on **this link** to do so now.

If you're still reading, you likely have not clicked the link. Uncon-vinced? Fearful of adding more spam to an inbox already bursting with suspicious pleas from family members stranded in Impact Zones they should definitely not be visiting? Don't worry: Unicorn Investments' newsletters are no carnival barker's cry trying to sell consignment carbon credits for pennies on the dollar.

Here's a sneak preview of what you'll get if you subscribe:

Special Situation: Wearables
Check your portfolio, Jeff: do you see any investments in Invasive Biometric Wearables? If so, congratulations—and welcome to the RA world. IBW startups are huge. Take Portable Physician's insane $304M round in Q3. The feared "blush factor" has not materialized for PP's ColonStatus skin patch monitor for those dealing with intestinal distress. And don't sleep on its smart mic microchip implant, Tonal, which harnesses the power of AI to monitor vocal inflection, tone, potential microaggressions, and suggestive cadence, and might put HR departments out of business.

What's Next for the Home Insurance Industry?
In short: collapse. Are you tied up in these stocks, Jeff? If so, your net worth might be as underwater as Miami Beach. With premiums and sea level rising, this sector is nuclear waste, only more radioactive.

Renewables Sub-Sector Faltering
The only reliably strong industry post–climate change impact has, of course, been Renewables. But since last week's release of IPCC's latest report confirming a 3.5-degree rise in global temperature, Renewables stocks have plummeted, leaving the industry in disarray and mutual fund managers scratching their heads. With the feared doomsday scenario confirmed, investors are stuck in a what's-the-point mentality. This massive sell-off provides RAs a rare opportunity to snatch up valuable stocks that are sure to roar back once investors have absorbed and accepted the findings in the IPCC report. Jeff, if you simply confirm your subscription to Unicorn Investments' newsletter, you will receive hot stock tips based on deep understanding of today's complex investment landscape, including abandoned Renew-

ables stocks that will make you a fortune once investor confidence returns and the Fear and Greed Index stabilizes.

Shirk the Long-Term Asset Allocation Mix: Yes, We're Serious
Unicorn Investments is known for its contrarian sentiments, but this one may shock even our longtime devotees: it's time to dump your long-term asset allocations. It's becoming clear that investors no longer have the luxury of assuming a long-term horizon for earnings. Short-term is the name of the game for savvy stockwatchers. Want to know more? Click the link and confirm your subscription.
You're still reading, Jeff. Why won't you click the link? Skeptical? Good. So are we, which is why we spent extra time analyzing this sizzling tip before passing it on to you:

Looser Regulation + Epidemic Mental Illness = $$$$
While rage-farmers, politicians, and talking heads bicker about whether solastalgia is a hoax or a real disease, biotech firms are racing to develop a cure. Although multiple clinical trial shutdowns have made beta investors skittish, we're hearing good things about Vortex Biologics' solastalgia drug, still in Phase 1 trials. I know what you're going to say, Jeff: Phase 1 is way too early to tell. Finish Phase 3 and then call me. Well, guess what, Jeff? By then it will be too late, because this gravy train is already pulling out of the station. Unicorn Investments' impeccable sources are confident that Vortex is sitting on a landmark medicine. Would you fold four of a kind because you're worried about a straight flush? Impress your friends with your dedication to improving health outcomes. They don't need to know you're making bank.

Jeff, PLEASE CONFIRM YOUR SUBSCRIPTION, and Unlock the Door to Staggering Impact-Immune Profits.™

THREE RIVERS PARK DISTRICT CLASS DESCRIPTION

"New Friends at the Feeder"

Having a hard time identifying the new feathered friends at your birdfeeder? Can't tell a keen-billed toucan from a Nicaraguan seed finch—and wouldn't know what to feed it if you did?

Increased biodiversity at Minnesota's birdfeeders is one of the few upsides to massive global climate change, but the now-seasonal arrival of mixed-species flocks from the southern hemisphere poses unique challenges to the midwestern birdwatcher. "New Friends at the Feeder" offers armchair enthusiasts a chance to learn all about these "new-to-us" critters in a low-stress environment. Topics covered include:

- How to avoid those bloody squabbles between squirrels and swallow-tailed kites at your groundfeeder
- Why tube feeders may not be up to the task of serving larger-bodied species, such as macaws
- Building "feeding zones" so aggressive flocks of tropical birds can be serviced separately from Minnesota legacy species that have not yet moved into southern Canada
- Learning how to live with the destructive habits of large birds

- Protecting your pets from new world parrots
- Adjusting to the chaos of hybrid flocks
- Coping with the feelings of anger, loss, and despair that come with the disappearance of familiar childhood species, such as cardinals and blue jays

Plus, you'll walk out of class with your own homemade coconut Tiki Bar parrot toy.

From the broad-billed motmot to the fiery-throated hummingbird, this class will help you adapt to and even learn to enjoy our new native birds.

**Please note that the info session for the three-day "Birding at Superfund Sites, Abandoned Nuclear Plants, and Evacuated Coastal Cities" guided tour has been changed to January 9.

"INCIDENT ON YELLOWSTONE TRAIL"

Climate Crime Files Podcast, Episode 276

JEN: Today's episode of Climate Crime Files is brought to you by Impact Cruises. Guys, you know that I'm literally obsessed with travel—like inappropriately obsessed to the point of it just being weird and uncomfortable for everyone. But some of the cities on my bucket list are kinda hard to get to these days. I mean, I'd basically given up on ever seeing the former site of New Orleans. And what was the point of hitting Miami after Terminal Submersion? Yeah, like most of you, I'd just written them off, super mad at myself for not checking these boxes off before rising sea levels gobbled them up. But then I found out about Impact Cruises' Endangered Cities 7-Day Free-Sail Cruise, and—oh my god, Steph, I literally just got goosebumps when I said that. Anyway, I found out about it, I booked it, it was life-changing, and I could not recommend it more. I got to see the floating artificial islands of Miami, sail around downtown Savannah—that was a big bucket list box I was able to check off—and even got to touch the top of St. Louis Cathedral in New Orleans. Steph, I snorkeled the South Beach Artificial Reef. But here's the deal: you gotta move now. These cities will officially become Restricted Impact Territorial Zones next year, so guys—

now is the time to treat yourself to the opportunity to take one last look at some of our most awesome vanished coastal cities while experiencing all the luxury you've come to expect from Impact Cruises. Use the promo code *climatecrimesfan* to get 30 percent off. Now, on to the show.

[dark audio sting]

JEN: On the afternoon of June 18, 2019, in a suburb outside Minneapolis, Ashley Shelby walked out into her back garden to pick some raspberries. She and her family lived in a super-old farmhouse that had been settled by French-Swiss immigrants who'd planted apple trees and raised dairy cows. Steph, the original barn was still on the property and there was a bunch of old rusted farm equipment still in it.

STEPH: Okay, I'm in love and not even afraid to leave my husband for her barn at this point, sight unseen.

JEN: Ashley's property had about an acre's worth of mixed forest. There were trees everywhere and a lot of them were crazy-old, including this enormous one that was growing on the northwest edge of the raspberry patch. Now, if you were to look at a picture of this tree before all this happened, you would basically be like *meh.* I mean, yes, it was really tall—reports later stated that it was seventy feet—but that was pretty much all it had to recommend itself. Ashley didn't really know what kind of tree it was, but, hey, it was her tree and she loved it. But something was really wrong with this tree. Ashley had been noticing for a while that it looked sick. And Steph, I'm going to post this picture on the website, but look at this photo that was taken of the tree around this time.

STEPH: Oh my god. It's like a skeleton. That is so disturbing.

JEN: And bear in mind, this was summer. So obviously Ashley had been noticing this, but she thought, hey, you know, maybe it's just having a hard year. Trees can get sick, just like people, but then they recover. Sometimes when a tree is cut down, you'll see a blip on the rings, and it's like kind of a patient history: oh, the tree was sick this year so the ring is super-skinny, or hey, there was a fire that year and the ring is funky-looking. Anyway, that day in the raspberry patch, Ashley was like, okay, this has been going on for long enough that I'm getting worried. I need to call somebody to see what's up.

[intense audio bed]

JEN: Now, what Ashley didn't know, and what no one saw coming, was that the tree was already dead. And when officials dug into this, they would learn things that would shake them to their very core.
STEPH: This is already terrifying, Jen.
JEN: Steph, it gets even creepier. Ashley had gone up to the tree and was inspecting the bark, kind of trying to see if she could find any clues there about why the tree looked so bad. Now, if you look closely at the picture on our website, you can see this kind of tree has super rough bark. Ashley is not a tree expert but she has a tree identification book in her bathroom—
STEPH: She keeps a tree identification guide on the back of her toilet? That is straight-up nerd bathroom reading.
JEN: Obviously. But it helped her figure out that this big old tree was some kind of ash. So she's looking and she notices a loose piece of bark, and when she removes it—Steph, when she removes it, she sees something that will turn this case upside down.

[dark audio sting]

JEN: When Ashley pulls the piece of bark from the tree, she sees all these weird, twisty engravings in the wood, and this sawdust-like fluff. So, Steph, I'm just going to read right from the arborist's report: "At time of initial assessment, the tree had been completely defoliated. Its bark had split and was marked by vertical fissures due to callous tissue formation. Upon removal of a section of bark, the homeowner observed serpentine galleries indicative of larval feeding, along with frass—a mix of sawdust and borer excrement."
STEPH: Ew.
JEN: "While manner of death should be determined by a state forester, this tree appears to have died from infection."

STEPH: Okay, I don't even totally understand most of what you said, but it sounds bad.

JEN: It *was* bad. The tree was dead, and it wasn't from natural causes, or even an accident. Something killed it. So, the arborist asks Ashley if she'd noticed any woodpeckers around.

STEPH: Uh, random.

JEN: That's what Ashley thought at first, too, but then she remembers that, yeah, over the past couple of years she's been noticing an unusually high number of woodpeckers around the property. In one account, she actually refers to them as "flocks."

STEPH: Oh my god, the thought of woodpeckers flocking is bone-chilling. Like, Hitchcockian.

JEN: Now, what no one knew yet was that the woodpeckers had descended onto her property not just because the tree was dying but because of what was *in* the tree.

STEPH: Now you're scaring me, Jen. What was in the tree?

JEN: A serial killer, Steph—one small enough to fit on a penny but powerful enough to take down entire forests. Some say powerful enough to take down an entire species of tree.

STEPH: I'm literally shaking right now.

JEN: Are you ready for this name? The Emerald Ash Borer.

STEPH: Okay, that almost sounds pretty. What is it?

JEN: They *are* pretty—like so pretty you kinda want to wear them as earrings. Except Emerald Ash Borer is an insect. I've posted a picture on the website so you can get a look.

STEPH: I'm looking at it right now, Jen. I know it's a bug and everything, but it's beautiful. Like, its wings look like they've been soaked in glitter. I feel like I've seen this on an Etsy necklace.

JEN: It's beautiful, but destructive. These bad boys are tiny, but they can slaughter an entire forest stand of ash trees within six years. And by the time they'd infected Ashley's tree, they'd graduated to mass murder—tens of millions of ash trees had been killed by these six-legged criminals. And they're not nice about it, Steph. They asphyxiate the tree.

STEPH: How does a tree asphyxiate?

JEN: I had the same question, so I did some research on this. What I found out kept me up all night. I guess the best way to explain what a tree experiences when Emerald Ash Borers cut through its tissues the way they do is to think about how it would feel if all your blood vessels and veins were severed. That's how to asphyxiate a tree.

STEPH: Jen, I can't even.

JEN: Now, we've reached the point in the story where things really get strange. It's what happened when the body was removed from Ashley's property. What should've been a somber but straightforward task turned into an operation that was so disturbing that to this day, Ashley won't talk about it. Stay tuned.

[commercial break]

[JEN—advertisement]: Longtime listeners know that, like so many others, I struggle with solastalgia, the suite of mental and emotional disorders brought on by active and predicted climate change impacts. And while talk therapy does help, I still sometimes experience episodes of rage, forgetfulness, week-long depressive episodes, retroactive climate denial, even catatonia. Your basic solastalgia experience. But then my doctor suggested Climafeel, and my life changed completely. Taken once a day, Climafeel offers solastalgia sufferers the ability to face a changing world with fearlessness and stress immunity while retaining the emotional versatility needed to experience love, happiness, and, of course, hope. Since starting a course of Climafeel, my episodes have been cut in half. Instead of waking up in a state of fear and anxiety, I feel optimistic for the first time in years. It's changed my outlook and provided me with the hope I need to wake up in the morning. In a world made strange—in a world defined by loss, a world that makes hope hard to come by . . . Climafeel can help. Now, back to the show.

[intense audio bed begins]

JEN: At this point, there is concern that the tree, even though dead as a doornail, might be infectious, putting nearby trees at risk. So Ashley does the responsible thing and hires a tree removal company. Now, when these tree people first came out to look at the crime scene and write up a bid to remove the body, they'd been super gentle and respectful when inspecting this old friend that Ashley had loved so much.

STEPH: As you would expect.

JEN: Exactly. No points given here for being decent. But the day the machines show up, things could not have been more different. Ashley's up in her office when she hears the roar of trucks coming up her gravel driveway—and then onto her lawn. It was a convoy—like way more e-F150s than should be legal. Then came the hydraulic crane, and it just sort of careens through Ashley's perennial gardens to get to the crime scene. The workers get into hard hats and saddles and start climbing the trunk of the dead tree, suspended by pulleys and ropes, and it begins. They begin to draw and quarter this tree, like it isn't someone's loved one—like it's nothing. They shear large limbs from the trunk with obnoxiously loud chainsaws. When the pith connecting a limb to the trunk gave way, it sounds like a bone breaking. It was that disturbing.

STEPH: Ew. I mean, I've never had to take a tree down—you know me, farm girl, I just wait until the trees fall down on their own. But that just sounds awful.

JEN: Right. So Ashley's up her in office, which overlooks the whole situation, and she's just trying to get some work done, so she closes the curtains and puts on her noise-canceling headphones. But the headphones can't cancel out the sound she hears next. It makes her blood run cold.

STEPH: Oh my god. What did she hear?

JEN: Are you ready for this?

STEPH: No, obviously.

JEN: It's laughter. She hears maniacal, insane laughter. Like, the kind you hear from movie villains. Ashley gets up and looks out the window just in time to see . . . get this . . . two *squirrels*, crazed with fear, running up the delimbed trunk, away from the workers and their chainsaws. Who are laughing like it's the funniest thing they've ever seen.

STEPH: No!

JEN: Yes. Steph, you've known me forever, and you know that, with the help of Climafeel, I can handle all the death and destruction, the climate-induced mass migration, refugee crises, and terminal submersions, but mess with a defenseless animal, and I'm coming for you.

STEPH: Obvs.

JEN: According to published reports, as the squirrels circled around the trunk frantically, the dudes with the chainsaws were getting closer and closer, like they can't even wait two seconds to bring the trunk down. With absolutely nowhere to go, both squirrels jump off the top of the seventy-foot tree.

STEPH: Oh. My. God. Oh my god, Jen! I'm literally shaking with rage right now. Did they survive?

JEN: So I've read conflicting reports on this, but most agree that Ashley raced downstairs and out into the adjoining forest where she thought the squirrels might've landed, but she found no sign of them. Later, she went online and did some research about squirrels that made her think that they might have survived. I guess squirrels can survive long jumps like that—I don't know. But there was bad news that no one saw coming: there had been a nest in that tree, and later, after everything, they found . . . I can't even say it, Steph.

STEPH: What, Jen? Oh, god—what did they find?

JEN: Three dead baby squirrels.

STEPH: *[sobs]*

JEN: Now, in the days that followed, Ashley's twelve-year-old son kept asking how such a teensy tiny insect could kill a giant tree. She tried to explain the concept of an invasive species to him, and, Steph, he asked her a question that stopped me dead in my tracks. He asked his mom: "Are *we* an invasive species?"

STEPH: Whoa.

JEN: Right? Ashley was totally taken aback. Like, *shook*. So she and her son looked up the scientific definition of invasive species and learned it is defined as, and I quote, "an organism not indigenous or native to a particular area and which causes great environmental harm to the new area—and to be considered invasive, a species must adapt, reproduce quickly, harm native plants and animals, thrive because there are no predators, and destroy habitat." Who does that sound like, Steph?

STEPH: Holy cow. That's . . . that's us, Jen.

JEN: Ashley's son felt the same way. He told her that going by that definition, *they* were invasive. And if they were invasive, then they were responsible for the death of the tree.

STEPH: I just got full-body chills.

JEN: Now, being a mother, Ashley assured her son that he had done nothing to cause the death of the tree, that it had been unlucky that the Emerald Ash Borer had decided to invade their tree—all the things you try to tell your kids when life is sucking hard. But then a week later, Ashley received a piece of information that would make her question everything that had happened up until this point— the criminal responsible for the tree's murder was not who they thought it was. It went much higher than the Emerald Ash Borer. It went all the way to the top.

STEPH: A mob hit?

JEN: If you consider humanity itself a mafia. In the report Ashley received from the state forester, she learned that while the Emerald Ash Borer infestation was the acute cause of the tree's death, it had been the victim of a more widespread crime syndicate engaged in human-assisted biological invasion due to human-caused climate change.

STEPH: Like, I'm not even sure what that all means but I hear the word *human* in that, like, twice.

JEN: It means that the agent of death—in this case, the Emerald Ash Borer—had been transmitted via shipping channels, like the ice-free Northwest Passage, which is basically Grand Central Station at this point. And because the insect thrives in the warmer winters that no longer get cold enough to kill off the insect larvae, the tree's death was preventable. I mean, the warmer winters are our fault, right, so this means humans had a role in the crime. It means that, at least in Ashley's mind, her son was right—that as a carbon user and emitter, she had played a role in the death of her favorite tree.

STEPH: It's like a version of "the call came from inside the house."

JEN: Exactly. And we can tell her that it's not her fault, that she can't buy into the lie the climate criminals and the energy oligarchs, the do-nothing legislators, and the fossil fuel companies still try to feed us, that we're responsible for all this and not them, but it doesn't matter. Like so many of us who grew up during Impact, that message of guilt and personal responsiblity is part of her DNA. And for her, there's no closure. Especially because this crime is expected to happen again and again, as billions of ash trees are expected to die the same way Ashley's tree died. This crime scene is going to replicate itself billions of times. Maybe there's no closure for any of us. Maybe all of us are dealing with the changes in the best ways we know how—whether that's planting seedlings of climate-resistant species, as Ashley and her family have been doing, taking advantage of pharmaceuticals like Climafeel to help us cope, binge-watching *Non-Preppers of the Pacific Northwest*—Steph, I'm looking at you—or doing podcasts like this.

STEPH: Amen.

[closing theme begins]

JEN: You can find all source material used in the show, including pictures of Ashley's tree and the report from the state on the tree's cause of death, on our website. Next week, we look into a case you guys have been begging us to cover for months: the Mystery of the Divorcing Albatrosses. These monogamous birds are known for their Hallmarkian love stories—they grow old together!

STEPH: Aw!

JEN: But something is changing on the Falklands: the divorce rate among these faithful birds is skyrocketing.

STEPH: No! We need at least one species that knows how to make relationships last!

JEN: But what researchers never saw coming was the reason behind all this avian heartbreak.

STEPH: Let me guess: another climate crime?

JEN: Exactly. That's next week on Climate Crime Files. Until then, Stay Vigilant, Stay Hopeful, and Remember: We *Can* Make Things Right.™

FEDERAL ELIGIBILITY QUESTIONNAIRE FROM THE TEMPORARY AID TO CLIMATE-IMPACTED DESERVING POOR BENEFITS PROGRAM

Eligible Impacted individuals who have been granted Designated Pauper status may receive up to three months of federally funded carbon credits, food vouchers, and housing assistance under the Temporary Aid to the Climate-Impacted Deserving Poor Benefits Program. All applicants must have a Domestic Climate Refugee Resettlement Number (DCRRN) and be registered with the U.S. Environmental Migrant Management Agency. *This form must be filled out in the presence of a Citizen Anti-Fraud Monitor and notarized.* All answers are Yes/No and must be answered truthfully under penalty of perjury.

1. Are you a citizen of the United States?

If No, do not continue.

2. Have you been convicted of a felony?

If Yes, do not continue.

3. **Do you have a score at or above +5 on the federally mandated Albrecht Solastalgia Screener?**

If Yes, notify the Citizen Monitor by raising both hands above your head. You will be given further instruction. If you are not in compliance with this federal regulation, do not continue.

4. **Did you complete the required education module "Protect Your Children By Not Having Them"?**

If you answered No, do not continue and see the Citizen Monitor for further instruction.

5. **Are you or have you ever been involved with any of the following subgroups of Late-Stage Climate Change Deniers:**

- Rapture Denier (you believed climate change was real but that it was caused by God or another deity or supernatural being)

- Compensated Denier (you received payment, gifts, or favors for arguing that "natural variation," "solar flares," or "volcanic disturbances" were responsible for climate changes or that climate change was not occurring at all)

- Legacy Denier (you were psychologically damaged by the cognitive dissonance resulting from decades of far-right media indoctrination, closely followed by the catastrophic effects of First Impact and can provide documentation of such from a licensed therapist)

If Yes to Rapture Denier or Compensated Denier, do not continue; you are not eligible for this program. If Yes to Legacy Denier, see Citizen Monitor for additional paperwork before continuing.

6. **Do you have a food-producing garden (windowsill garden, rooftop garden, backyard garden, or a plot in a community garden)?**

If Yes, continue. If No, continue. (This is a demographic question that has no bearing on your eligibility.)

7. Do you agree with the following statement: "The welfare of each Impacted individual would best be promoted by having them solve their own problems through normal banking and commercial channels?"

If Yes, continue. If No, see the Citizen Monitor for reeducation materials before continuing.

When you have completed this form, please bring it to the Citizen Anti-Fraud Monitor, who will notarize it and provide you with the application form (if eligible). Please note that benefits are not guaranteed and are granted at the discretion of the Environmental Migrant Management Agency. Citizenship status, criminal background, and the applicant's Personal Documented Climate Change Rhetoric Score will be assessed by the Domestic Refugee Solutions Committee in conjunction with your application. Please note: there is no appeal process.

ERSATZ CAFÉ MENU (STORE #350)

We are pleased to reopen under new management following Superstorm XY and the catastrophic failure of the Bridging Berm protecting the Lower East Side. We appreciated all the support—and helping hands—as we moved operations to Manhattan's Habitable Zone, transforming this vacant laundromat under the old 155th Street Viaduct into a friendly Ersatz Café franchise location.

"COFFEE" DRINKS
A friendly reminder: due to the simultaneous and total collapse of both the African and South American Arabica crops last year, *coffee* is used as a term of convenience and does not necessarily refer to coffee as we previously understood it.

Ground Acorn and Carob Mocha
We rely on the region's best bushcrafters for the nuts used in our Organic Acorn Espresso. Paired with Hershey's carbon-neutral carob powder, this decadent brew will cheer even the crankiest former coffee lover.

Postum Speedball
For customers currently experiencing Forced Caffeine Transition Syndrome, our Postum Speedball can ease the discomfort of climate-

driven withdrawal. This creamy Postum drink is blended with a half-shot of our limited hydroponic-cultivated Robusta bean espresso. A note from your medical provider is required for purchase due to limited bean supplies.

Chicory and Chickpea Coffee-Like Drink
Percolated to perfection, our ground chickpea steamer will spark pre-Impact latté nostalgia. We brighten this steamer with the piquancy of a wild chicory shot and a cloud of cashew-based "whipped cream."

First-Year Burdock Root House Blend
For our bold new house blend, we roast tender first-year burdock roots for ten hours to draw out their dramatic flavor. Our burdock is raised by carbon felons in the Manhattan Comprehensive Sanction Center's community garden and comes to your cup with a dollop of social responsibility.

Second-Run House Blend
Some former coffee fiends believe the second pot made from a basket of burdock root grounds has a subtler mouthfeel. Plus, it's half-price.

SALADS
Ersatz Café is proud to be a part of the New York Invasive Species Salads Initiative and offers a daily special based on what our dedicated Foraging Specialist brings in each day. Typical greens include Bastard Cabbage, Sow's Thistle, Garlic Mustard, and Lamb's Quarters. Ask for today's salad selections, and please ensure your Release of Liability form is on file before ordering.

SWEETS 'N' SAVORIES
As the New York City Department of Climate Conversion continues its audit of Approved Climate-Transitional Foodstuffs for Commercial Sale, we are still offering only a limited lunch menu. These items have been sanctioned by the department's Committee on Low-Impact Substitutes of Unavailable Comestibles.

Dandelion Flower Risotto

One upside to exploding levels of carbon dioxide has been the veritable sea of dandelions across the country. Our savory cauliflower risotto is made from free-range dandelions harvested from New York's greenest rights-of-way and freeway shoulders. Served with hearth-baked nettle chips.

Saddle of Squirrel in Merlot Sauce

An intriguing transition meat, squirrel offers the discerning palate frank flavor with a presentation that doesn't test the gag reflex. Long and slow is the way to go with any ground rodent, and that's how we start. Slow-cooked for two days in a heady broth of locally sourced elderberries and organic bathtub gin, our humanely trapped squirrels are served on a bed of climate-smart sorghum pilaf studded with birch-harvested Chaga mushrooms.

Forager's Surprise

Comfort food has become harder and harder to find since First Impact, but this wild-crafted casserole is sure to soothe and console. Caramelized chickweed melds with milky cap mushrooms and wild yams to produce a toothsome dish that heals all the hurts.

Wood Sorrel and Mexican Wasp Honey Sorbet

With sorrel harvested from our own rooftop garden and honey sourced from the New Jersey Mexican Honey Wasp Apiary, this delicious sorbet creates an earthy yet succulent flavor bomb. It arrives at your table with a light carbon footprint and a calorie count under 100.

Cave-Matured Zucchini Cheese Plate

The nationalization of the American dairy industry under the Selective Reduction of Methane-Emitting Livestock Act doesn't have to mean the end of your cheese adventures. Give our selection of heirloom zucchini cheeses the old college try. From the wild ramp and garlic faux Manchego to our cranberry-infused pea milk Gouda, indulge in the visceral joy of consuming cheese without the fear of hefty fines.

DIETARY CONCERNS

We do our utmost to accommodate allergies and food restrictions. Please be aware of current city, state, and federal laws regarding food consumption and/or associated carbon tax upcharges for certain climate-sensitive foods. We will not accommodate Paleo or Keto requests due to the global moratorium on methane-producing livestock (and no, we don't "know a guy").

VIOLENT BIOPHILIA IN SOLASTALGIA PATIENTS

Case Study

Claire Peake, Ph.D.

Environmental Epidemiology, 28 May 2038:
Volume 422, Issue 6122, eabg4020
DOI: 12.2126/science.abg4020

NARRATIVE

In late 2032, in a psychiatric hospital near Madrid specializing in late-stage *solastalgia*—an umbrella term coined by G. Albrecht et al.[1] describing the human emotional response to active and predicted climate change impacts—a series of unusual events unfolded. These events commenced with a single complaint from a thirty-four-year-old male patient about a painting that hung on the wall of his private room. When interviewed later, his day nurse recollected that the patient's complaint was nonspecific, so she did not make a note of it

---

1. Albrecht, G., G.-M. Sartore, L. Connor, N. Higginbotham, S. Freeman, B. Kelly, G. Pollard, et al. (2007). "Solastalgia: The Distress Caused by Environmental Change." *Australasian Psychiatry* 15 (l_suppl), S95–S98. https://doi.org /10.1080/10398560701701288.

on his chart or discuss his complaint with other hospital staff. Three days later, the patient destroyed the painting.

The piece in question was an inexpensive abstract print from Ikea featuring broken blue and black lines and rugged brush strokes. It was titled "Sky." The artist was uncredited. Some of the staff, unaware of the painting's title, later told researchers that it had depicted either a cave or some sort of storm.[2]

Over the next two weeks, hospital staff received more patient complaints regarding framed art in the facility. Severe *solastalgia* made interviews of the complainants difficult due to the disease's hallmark malaise, pervasive despair, and episodic catatonia. However, one patient, a sixty-three-year-old man from the drought-struck western United States, stated that the painting in his room, which featured curving black lines and blended ink splats, was "strangling" him. Several patients told their nurses that the art in their rooms had been intentionally chosen by the doctors to surveil their thoughts. A twenty-six-year-old environmental refugee from Turkey put her foot through a painting consisting of a chaotic blend of harsh orange and red brushstrokes, telling staffers that the painting had been "siphoning" her thoughts and "regurgitating" them.[3]

Although these incidents were discussed at weekly staff meetings, no action steps were taken until the frequency of the attacks increased dramatically. This happened quickly. By the end of the month seventeen paintings had gone missing. Those eventually located were found in a state of ruin. Some had been torn by hand (scissors being unattainable in the facility), while others had been desecrated by bodily fluids. Doctors found it curious that in many cases adjacent artwork had been left untouched. This phenomenon repeated itself in common areas of the facility as well. However, the medical staff could

---

2. One orderly commented that it looked like a "bad bruise."

3. When contacted by researchers, the Swiss artist who had licensed the painting to Ikea said the aim of that specific piece was to convey emotion without specific imagery.

find nothing to link the assaults and began to consider the possibility of mass psychogenic illness (MPI).

Frustrated, the hospital director instructed the janitorial staff to remove all art from the walls of the facility. Before this could happen, however, a custodian pointed out that the artwork that had been spared appeared to be realistic depictions of Nature. A stand of birch in one case. A naturalistic study of a seascape in another. A large panoramic photograph of a Canadian aspen grove survived a particularly violent attack in the cafeteria in which seven paintings were damaged.

The pieces that had been attacked were now reexamined, and it quickly became clear that the targeted paintings could all be classified as abstract. The hospital director instructed staff to replace all remaining "abstract" paintings in the facility with representative depictions of Nature—an act that dovetailed with an existing biophilic design initiative currently underway at the facility. After this was completed, there were no other reported attacks on artwork at this facility.

DISCUSSION

As defined by Erich Fromm and developed by E. O. Wilson and other scholars, *biophilia* encompasses the simple idea that human beings have a fundamental and genetically based need for and propensity to affiliate with other life forms. Using an illustrative example commonly used to describe biophilia, when given a choice between interacting with a rock or an ant, nearly all very young children will follow the ant.

Considered imprecise and unprovable by the scientific community pre-Impact, the relatively recent discovery of the *biophilia* genetic marker has led to a medical understanding of the fundamental human need for contact with Nature and the development and use of biophilic design in hospitals, prisons, and schools.

Now recognized by some scholars as part of a taxonomy of fundamental human needs, *biophilia* is so imbedded in the human consciousness and so critical to emotional and mental well-being that

researchers have demonstrated that it can be satisfied even with rep-
resentations of natural scenes, such as photographs and paintings.

However, the events that unfolded at this psychiatric hospital
offer a real-world and somewhat novel opportunity to test Kaplan
and Kaplan's Model of Environmental Preference, which argues that
in addition to mystery, coherence, and complexity, humans require
"legibility" in their environments.[4] In this case, it was the lack of legibility that appeared to cause distress in the patients, all of whom had,
in addition to their solastalgia diagnoses, suffered from a disordered
biophilic drive.

While legibility is not a primary goal of abstract art, legibility *is*
something the *solastalgia*-struck often lack and are therefore com-
pulsively driven to find in a world warped and made strange by climate change. (It is important to note, however, that this drive can
be seen in many climate-impacted individuals who have not been
diagnosed with *solastalgia*.)

At the same time, the Kaplans have also found that a quality
widely referred to as "mystery" is important to human interaction
with Nature. Mystery, in this sense, can be defined by features such
as foliage-obscured vistas, coiling brooks, and winding paths. (Where
art depicting Nature and this narrowly defined version of "mystery"
stop and abstraction begins is worthy of deeper analysis but is beyond
the scope of this paper.)

Finally, although the literature currently offers scant few examples
of the consequences of disruption of the biophilic drive, researchers
have been tracking the violent escalation of this drive when access to
outlets have been limited or when the outlets themselves have been
warped. It is with substantial circumspection, then, that I classify the
events described above as another example of this kind of escalation
and, in fact, propose a new term to describe these behaviors: *Violent
Biophilia.*

---

4. Kaplan, R., and S. Kaplan. (1989). *The Experience of Nature: A Psychological
Perspective.* Cambridge, U.K.: Cambridge University Press.

DOCUMENTS (RECOVERED)   85

CONCLUSION/RECOMMENDATIONS

Understanding the relationship between biophilia and the most widely diagnosed biophilic pathology, *solastalgia*, is a formidable challenge facing social scientists and medical professionals today. The interior nature of other mental disorders makes them easier to treat, even those with a biologic provenance. Mild or early-stage environmental melancholia, on the other hand, is triggered and further aggravated by exterior existential causes, ranging from acute disaster experiences and forced migration to more generalized loss, including loss of familiar habitat and foodstuffs, the absence of clearly delineated seasons, disrupted bird migration patterns, etc. As such, it requires aggressive treatment to keep it from advancing to solastalgia.

Described by Albrecht et al. as being akin to "homesickness you have when you are still at home," solastalgia sometimes responds to a delicate blend of nostalgia therapy, distress tolerance training, and broad-based consolation activities using the current SRC therapeutic approach to solastalgia and solastalgia-adjacent illnesses: Salvage (what you can), Rebuild (what you are able), Console (yourself and others).

In recent years, biopharmaceutical firms have begun developing "anti-solastalgia" drugs in an effort to mitigate, palliate, or, in one case,[5] "cure" the grief and distress experienced by human beings due to the loss—both actual and anticipated—of natural environments. However, the consensus among solastalgia researchers in the fields of epidemiology, etiology, medicine, and mental health is clear: no pharmaceutical or biopharmaceutical intervention is likely to treat a disease that is biophilic in origin, unless the intervention alters or destroys the biophilic drive. And without the biophilic drive, without the fundamental need for nature, one might be forgiven for asking if we can even call ourselves human.

---

5. Vortex Biologics' Climafeel.

CLIMAFEEL IN-HOUSE MARKETING BRIEF

[Vortex Biologics]

PRODUCT DETAILS

Climafeel: a recombinant DNA biologic that blunts the effects of solastalgia, utilizing the genetically modified Taq1 A1 allele on the ANKK1 gene (psychopathy/antisocial disorder[1] polymorphism).

Disease Treated: Solastalgia

Solastalgia refers to a suite of environmental illnesses, mostly psychiatric but including some physical disorders, thought to be caused by climate-related changes to the natural world, as well as related impacts on built environments (homes, neighborhoods, and cities). Symptoms of classic solastalgia include major depression, dysthemia, depressive psychosis, severe anxiety, and panic disorders that escalate to any of the following:

- episodic catatonia
- excessive remembering
- retrospective rage episodes (intermittent or continuous)

---

1. Will be rebranded in all marketing materials and future media assets as Cleckley's Syndrome. See "Key Marketing Points" below.

- persistent despair
- retroactive climate denial (found mostly in high-impact communities)

Thanks to Vortex's Solastalgia Education Campaign initiative, last year's DSM revision included the official recognition of several subtypes of solastalgia as discrete disorders:

- Dolittle Phenomenon[2] (hearing animals speaking)
- Natural Disaster Dissociative Disorder (disaster-induced serial fugue states)
- Environmental Hyperempathy (tree-based mirror-touch synesthesia)
- Solastalgia-Induced Apotemnophilia (elective amputation)

Expected Outcomes

Climafeel is expected to provide broadly effective treatment of many solastalgia symptoms, effectively functioning as full restoration of health ("cure") in many cases. Users should anticipate:

- upgraded adaptive abilities, particularly in moments of high stress (evacuations, displacement, migrant/refugee travel, long-term FEMA camp stays, and resource scarcity, including food riots, water conflicts, and steep financial losses due to volatile markets)
- decrease in emotional dysregulation and anxiety caused by actual, imagined, or potential climate-caused changes
- enhanced stress immunity
- increased tolerance of climate-impacted environments, including those held in universal esteem, such as the former Patagonian ice fields, islands in international Terminal Submersion Zones (Key West, Georgia's Tybee Island, North

---

2. Dening, T.R., and A. West. (1990). "The Doolittle Phenomenon: Hallucinatory Voices from Animals." *Psychopathology* 23(1): 40–45.

Carolina's Outer Banks, Solomon Islands, the Maldives, the
vanished Redwoods of Big Sur, the Arctic Memorial Economic
Opportunity Zone, etc.) and those associated with positive
private memories, including nostalgia-stimulating landscapes
that have disappeared or been "negatively" transformed by
climate-related changes

Side Effects
Cleckley's Syndrome (full expression). Movement dysfunction, including tremors. Constipation. Insomnia. These are not all the side effects.

MARKET ANALYSIS
With the supply of climate-induced pain in no danger of diminish-
ing, solastalgia diagnoses are projected to increase exponentially,
suggesting a robust and expanding market for Climafeel. In addition,
large-scale concerns about the disease's impact on the workforce
have contributed to recent instability in the labor market, specifically its devastating effect on labor force participation. After factoring
in comorbidities resulting in increased PTO, suicide-related loss of
institutional knowledge and the associated onboarding costs of new
hires, and diminished workplace productivity, solastalgia is costing
U.S. businesses nearly $400 billion a year. Pent-up corporate de-
mand for effective solastalgia treatments suggests several avenues
for partnerships, including sponsored employer-wellness programs
that could prove to be effective sales funnels.

Finally, the FDA's simultaneous approval of Climafeel as both
a treatment and a prophylaxis offers entry into other markets and
demographics, allowing Vortex to offer preventive care to individuals
who may benefit from prophylactic use of the drug, including pre-
solastalgic environmental refugees, the climate anxious, fire lookouts,
water miners, farmers, minority populations,[3] and children.

---

3. Indigenous communities, particularly circumpolar peoples (Inuit, Yupik,
Iñupiat), experience solastalgia at higher rates than the general population,
attributable to cataclysmic changes to their environments. However, early

Other Available Treatments
Solastalgia is a complex disease that is not known to respond to available psychotropics currently on the market. Antidepressants, stimulants, antipsychotics, and anxiolytics have not been shown to reduce symptoms and in some cases have worsened them. The use of palliative measures is the current standard of care for mid- to late-stage solastalgics, including exposure to available nonimpacted natural environments or exceedingly well-constructed biophilic simulations, such as those utilized in the moonglade hospice model. However, access to nonimpacted natural environments is obviously limited, and high-level bio-sims are out of reach for most consumers.

MARKETING CHALLENGES
Through genetic modification of polymorphism (Taq1 A1 allele on the ANKK1 gene and upregulation of protein-coding genes CDH5 and OPRD1), Vortex's world-class team of geneticists, research scientists, medicinal chemists, and microbiologists have leveraged cutting-edge pharmacogenomics to isolate the most adaptive traits associated with Cleckley's Syndrome, while eliminating most maladaptive aspects of the condition.

Solastalgia is, at its core, an inability or unwillingness to adapt to changed environmental circumstances. At the same time, adaptability is more important than ever. Research shows that "psychopathic" individuals have little difficulty dealing with the consequences of rapid change. In fact, they thrive on it. These individuals feel the "moral pinch" less keenly than others, a useful trait in moments requiring decisiveness. They do not understand or experience anxiety, for they experience far less fear of imagined and real catastrophic events than nonpsychopathic individuals. They are virtually immune to trauma and demonstrate resilience in the face of chaos, stress, and rapid change.

Climafeel focus group results indicate a strong resistance among these groups to pharmaceutical-based solutions to solastalgia. This is likely due to stubborn cultural beliefs and an animistic worldview that positions "Nature" as inseparable from human existence.

In a time of climate impact, these are adaptive traits.

Our clinical trials have shown that the upregulation of CDH5 and OPRD1, as well as the proprietary modification of the ANKK1 Taq1 A1 allele, as delivered by Climafeel, provides *therapeutic levels of psychopathy*. Vortex scientists have achieved this by:

- adjusting downward the MAOA polymorphism codes for risk and aggression
- eliminating fragility
- tempering the psychopathic aesthetic deficit so that books, art, films, etc. may be enjoyed or at least understood on an emotional level
- promoting detachment with room for reaction impulses to act positively
- modulating self-centered narcissism
- enhancing empathy capacity to approach socially adaptive levels
- removing Machiavellian tendencies while retaining the ability to design inventive solutions

There is no doubt that high levels of psychopathy, or psychopathic expression—cunning egocentricity, complete lack of empathy, blame externalization, etc.—are maladaptive. But so are low levels. Evidence shows that *intermediate* levels of psychopathy are adaptive, and perhaps even necessary now and in the years to come.

Climafeel will allow the solastalgic to move out of catatonic despair and into an adaptive, optimistic mindset in which a positive future is possible, all without the urge to manipulate or hurt others.

Overcoming "Repugnancy Cost"
Thoughtful market positioning and clear communication about how Climafeel works are crucial to overcoming the consumer's wisdom of repugnance, or "yuck factor." Any marketing campaign must convince consumers that psychopathy is a beneficial evolutionary adaption—an evolved life-history strategy that persists in our gene pool because

it is useful to society. At the same time, messaging must clearly convey that Vortex scientists have isolated and strengthened beneficial traits while muting the most problematic aspects. (Disease branding efforts—*Cleckley's Syndrome* rather than *psychopathy*—will be key to customer and provider buy-in.)

While some progress has been made in better understanding those with antisocial disorder, misconceptions still remain. The association of psychopaths with criminal behavior is a canard—70 to 90 percent of criminals, for example, are not psychopaths.[4] In reality, psychopaths occupy important roles in our society. They perform brain surgery. They run corporations. They govern. They lead military campaigns. Pro-social psychopaths contribute to the common good. Climafeel will harness these strengths and make them available to those who seek a way out of their disease and a way ahead in this challenging world.

Note: Search Term Management and Strategy will be key to public framing. Aggressive sponsorship of the following search terms and keywords will be necessary to control the narrative about Climafeel: *Climafeel prescription, Climafeel generic, Climafeel hope, Climafeel happy, Climafeel halflife, Climafeel withdrawal, Climafeel Illuminati, Climafeel psychopath, Climafeel evil, Climafeel dead inside.*

Key Marketing Points

- **Rebrand Psychopathy/Antisocial Personality Disorder as Cleckley's[5] Syndrome:** utilize lexical diplomacy to euphemize reference to antisocial personality disorder and psychopathy. Frame these as "legacy terms." Design and execute grassroots campaign to have disorder included in next DSM revision under this name, making destigmatization a key point. Refer to Pharmacia's Detrol campaign ("incontinence" to "overactive bladder") and GlaxoSmithKline's public awareness campaign for social anxiety drug Paxil (slogan: "Imagine Being Allergic to People").

---

4. In fact, criminals are more likely to suffer from a surfeit of emotions.
5. After Dr. Hervey M. Cleckley, the "father" of psychopathy.

- **Highlight the adaptive traits offered by Climafeel by contrasting them with the most salient symptoms of solastalgia:** provide potential consumers with a mental before-and-after picture of themselves by highlighting common solastalgia symptoms in conjunction with the benefits offered by Climafeel.

- **Create a sense of inevitability:** it's too late to stop the changes. They're here and they're only going to get worse. Consumers need to ask themselves how they want to exist in this world: as someone who succumbs to despair and disease or as someone who can adapt without hurting other people in the process.

- **Emotional appeal to consumers' "burden aversion":** no one wants to be a burden to their loved ones. Severe solastalgia requires round-the-clock care while milder cases typically result in unemployment and medical costs. Expenses can easily bankrupt families. Climafeel can reverse the effects of this debilitating disease. Key in on consumer's aversion to becoming a drain on family finances and emotions.

- **Moral appeal to family members' guilt:** for those caring for mid- to late-stage solastalgics who may harbor reluctance or repugnance toward Climafeel, pose the question, "Are you prepared to live with the fact that you could have done something that might have alleviated your loved one's pain but chose not to?"

Suggested Slogans from Vortex Drug Development Team

We can't put the world back together, but we can make it easier to be in the world.

You've carried the pain for too long. Let Climafeel shoulder the load.

Seamless adaptation is possible with Climafeel.

Have you ever wondered what it might feel like not to care? Have you ever wished you didn't have to?

PARTICIPANT HISTORIES FROM THE CLIMAFEEL CLINICAL TRIAL

THE INGENIOUS FUTILITY OF WARBLERS

(Elizabeth Fugit)

Elizabeth "Bick" Fugit

Bloomington, Indiana

Diagnosis: DSM-7, 650.6: Environmental Illness, Solastalgia
[Dolittle Phenomenon]

2035

The first time a bird found Bick the screens were off the windows for spring cleaning. It landed on the sill. It had a yellow cap, gold-dusted feathers, and a wild eye. After rearranging its wings several times, the bird looked at Bick and began to sing. Within moments, it was joined by another bird, identical. After a brief pause, the birds took up the song together. They hopped madly; to Bick, it looked as if they were dancing. Bick's mother came in to see about the noise and calmly shooed the birds away. Bick returned to playing with her doll.

They came often that year, but spring cleaning was over and the screens were back on, so they clung to the black mesh with their tiny, twig-like talons and they sang and sang.

2038

Bick felt important. You did not see children on campus very often, her mother said as they approached the Department of Psychological and Brain Sciences. College campuses were for scholars, and scholars were usually adults, or near-adults, although sometimes you saw high school kids.

Her mother knew a lot about campus, knew where just about everything was. After her release from Twilight Cove four months earlier, she'd gotten a part-time job at Wells Library as a circulation specialist, where she maintained a courteous and professional attitude, provided directions, retrieved library materials for patrons from closed-stack areas, and performed other duties as assigned. This job was usually given to a student, but the Director of Library Services was a family friend who wanted to help.

Bick's father was already at the door, holding it open for them. He was impatient and vaguely upset. They were supposed to arrive fifteen minutes early for this appointment, but they were only eight minutes early.

Then Bick saw it. A stone sculpture set atop a metal column. A weird lump of gray imprinted with folds, coils, and seams. She thought it was ugly. It looked like a butt. She looked at her mother. "What is this supposed to be?"

"What do you think it is?"

She hesitated. "A wrinkly butt?"

The sound of her mother's laughter filled Bick with warmth. "It's a brain, silly. A model of the human brain." She gently tapped the top of Bick's head. "You've got one just like it in here." Then she tapped her own head. "I have one, too. It's where our thoughts live." How could such an ugly thing be inside them? Bick thought. How could such a disgusting blob contain the very thought that called itself disgusting?

"But why is there a statue of a brain here?"

"Stop dawdling," her father called from the door. "We're late."

"Because the people in this building do nothing but study the brain," Bick's mother replied. "Its being here tells everyone who walks by that this is where people study the brain. Sort of like how the music school might have a statue of a music note on its lawn."

"There must be something wrong with my brain if we're here," Bick said.

Her mother reached down and brushed Bick's bangs off her forehead with two fingers. "No, honey, there's nothing wrong with your brain. There's something wrong with the world. And it's just trying to tell someone who will listen."

"Jesus Christ," her father yelled. People passing by on the sidewalk turned to look.

There was a department's worth of residents and psychologists and professors and other interested parties in the room when the questioning began.

Do you hear voices, Elizabeth?

Of course I hear voices. I can hear your voice right now.

I mean, do you hear voices when no one else is around?

Like ghosts?

Any kind of voice that no one else can hear.

No.

What about the birds, Bick?

Everyone hears birds. Except deaf people, but maybe they hear them in a different way.

Yes, but you also hear them in a different way from everyone else, don't you?

How should I know?

Bick, you told your parents that the birds talk to you. How do they talk to you?

They just do, the same way they talk to each other.

They sing to you?

That's how birds talk. Everyone knows that.

Are the songs like a language?

Songs are words.

And you understand the songs?

I guess.

Do the birds tell you to do things?

No. They don't care what I do. They only come to me because I understand. They'd come to you, too, if you'd listen.

When did they start talking to you?

I don't remember.

And what do they say to you, Elizabeth?

Only one thing.

They only say one thing to you? All of them? All of them say the same thing?

Yup.

Okay. What do they say?

They just ask why.

2048

The golden-winged warbler appeared, just as it had every Monday morning for the past two months, when Bick sat by the window with her guitar. The professor's office had grown close; the windows were old and wouldn't open, having been painted over too many times. Bick's father was weeping again as the professor fumbled in her desk for tissues. While this weekly ritual unfolded, Bick looked out the window at the limestone brain and thought about her mother, who was fifty days into a 180-day stay at the Indiana State Hospital for the Environmentally Unwell.

"Everyone hears the voice of the natural world," her father told the professor as he wiped his nose. "Why do you people keep making that into a fatal disease?"

Bick gingerly worked the E minor pentatonic scale with her short fingers and watched the tiny nugget of yellow and gray as it settled on the sill. It had a black mask, a black bib, one sun-bright eye, and one clouded eye, a diplomat from a lost palatinate whose language no one except Bick understood.

The professor sighed. "As I've said, Mr. Fugit, we have much to learn about this disorder, but there is no indication yet that it is fatal. Her scans are clean—no signs of plaques. However, these sorts of environmental maladies are now thought to be manifestations of solastalgia. Untreated, your daughter could begin experiencing more serious delusions. Possibly psychosis. But there are promising treatments in the pipeline. One in particular might be a good fit for—"

"Not this again," her father spat. "I've done my own research. This so-called disease is a hoax. Solastalgia is a lie fabricated by Big Pharma and people like you trying to make a buck. How much do they pay you to push this hoax? It doesn't exist."

"Mr. Fugit. I know this is hard."

"Look, the kid likes Nature. Animals. Little birds. She thinks they're her friends."

"Your daughter says birds speak to her, a delusion that has persisted for nearly ten years. It's why you came to us in the first place. The presence of hallucinatory voices coming from animals, flowers, or bodies of water are a hallmark symptom of the disorder. This explains why none of the other interventions we've tried have worked. I had a client who said he heard thrushes talking, condemning him for something they would never specify. Later, he said a blackbird came and looked at him judgmentally."

By now, Bick knew that silence was always best, that fingerpicking a blues turnaround could pass for comment, but she couldn't stop herself from corroborating this fact. "Yes. Blackbirds are very judgy." The adults looked at her. "What happened to him? The man."

"A warbler told him to put bleach in his eyes."

"A warbler?"

"Yes."

"And did he do it?"

"Yes, he did," the professor replied grimly.

Bick let loose a huge laugh and returned to her fingerpicking.

"Why is that funny to you, Elizabeth?"

"Because he's a liar, and even though you guys think you're so smart, you believed him."

"He didn't lie, Elizabeth. I saw him in the hospital. He's blind."

"I'm not talking about the bleach. I'm talking about the bird. He lied about the bird."

"Why do you think he was lying about the bird?"

"Because a warbler wouldn't tell someone to do something like that. Never. A blackbird maybe, but not a warbler. He must have wanted to do it and just needed an excuse. I mean, it's less insane, right? Isn't it less insane to say a bird told you to pour bleach in your eyes than to admit you did it because you wanted to hurt yourself?" The professor said nothing. "People are like that, you know. People sometimes like to hurt themselves."

Bick's father walked around the table, took the guitar from her hands, and set it against the chair. Then he got to his knees and took both of Bick's hands. "You're the one who's lying, Bick. You've been lying about the birds since you were five. Maybe we didn't give you enough attention when you were little and this whole charade is how you get what you need. That's my fault. I know I've failed you in a million different ways, but I'm begging you. Please stop this."

A disfiguring silence fell upon them.

There was a flash of wings on the other side of the window and the small unblinking eye found her.

Why?

Her father's fist hit the window hard and a crack appeared like magic, running diagonally across the glass. "Leave her alone!" The professor opened the door and Bick heard the woman's hurried foot-steps echoing down the hall. The startled warbler flew off but then cir-cled back and danced in front of the window. Bick's father stumbled backward. His face was gray. Bick thought he might puke.

Then there were more footsteps in the hall and the sound of more doors opening. There were so many doors opening that Bick won-dered if it were possible that there were more doors than birds in the world.

People entered the room and surrounded her father, tending to him and speaking kindly, gently lowering him into a chair and offer-ing him water. Bick stood up and approached the window. The war-bler saw her and stopped dancing. Bick watched as it looped around the oak that shaded the front walk before landing on the great stone brain. Another warbler came. Then two more sailed down from an unseen refuge in the oak's canopy, followed by a group of five from the same spot. Flashes of gold illuminated the dark places in the tree like tiny yellow lanterns. More warblers came descending upon the statue and gaining purchase on the wrinkles and folds that Bick had once found so repulsive. Soon there were so many birds that the brain ceased to exist, replaced by a silent, vibrating roost.

Students on the path stopped to look. Those who had already passed by turned back. People hurried across the quad. Devices came out as the birds preened and stretched. People took photos and videos, and still more birds came, fitting themselves between those already there. They watched the window, waiting for Bick to explain. Things were not how they had always been. The world was different. Why? They wanted to know why. But though Bick heard their question, she could not answer it. They told her the world did not make sense, that it had changed, but this was the only world Bick knew and it made sense to her.

Her mother had once told her that birds come into existence already knowing how things are supposed to be, but Bick knew for a fact that kids didn't. Kids had to be taught these things. Maybe the things they'd been taught were wrong. Maybe the things they'd been told about the way the world had been and the way it was now had been nothing but lies. Probably Bick would never know how things were supposed to be, and maybe it was better that way.

Still, the birds had found her and they would keep asking why, maybe until she was old, maybe even until she was dead, but Bick couldn't answer because she didn't know why.

THEY DON'T TELL YOU WHERE TO PUT THE PAIN

(Winfield Scott)

Winfield Scott

Miami, Florida

Diagnosis: DSM-7, 650.9: Environmental Illness, Solastalgia
[environment-induced apotemnophilia]

2035

Miami's first massive submersion event: Hurricane Xerxes. Win, thirty-four, freshly disillusioned by the carbon-transition economy, stood with a couple of other fresh-faced "apprentices" on a Coconut Grove beach, watching a caravan of hydrogen-cell Jaguars and Mercedes SUVs drive off Indian Creek Island, grill to bumper, a high-net funeral procession across the 91st Street Bridge. They all knew they were going to be moving up in the world very shortly; there was no way Florida's billionaires were going to go gentle into eminent domain proceedings. And they didn't. Despite the mandatory evacuation and the condemnation of all island properties, the new oligarchs turned to the Caretakers, the ghosts of System D, to preserve their landed wealth, both above ground and underground. There still existed an unaccountable optimism that the sea would recede, that human ingenuity would wrangle the ruin human ingenuity had wrought.

Win was too old to be green, too new to be trusted. Two days earlier, the Guild man had looked askance at his résumé and his several useless degrees and the long list of jobs from the usual post-Impact financial sectors—vertical farming and hydroponic solutions, environmental migrant management, conservation finance, deep decarbonization. "Morgan Stanley?"

"Data aggregation. I'm not proud. Until I got wise, I was that fuckface on LinkedIn who'd write, 'Thirty years ago, five people were invited into Mark Zuckerberg's dorm room to discuss a business idea. Two showed up and became billionaires. Don't close yourself off to new ideas.' I made people think all their problems were about not 'being open.' The scales have fallen from my eyes, though, if that makes a difference."

"Guild says you saved a kid's life off Tybee during the last big one."

"Probably should've let him drown. Would've been kinder."

"Never know. He might end up being The One."

"Breeders been saying that for decades. None of their spawn's ever been The One yet."

The Guild man looked at him hard as flint. "You go to church?"

"Do you?"

"When there's a church handy."

"Then you must know that divine forgiveness must satisfy divine justice."

The Guild man stood up. "I don't like you. You still reek of capital. You'll turn tail and run if things get hard. They won't take to you; you won't fit in." He set his Device down on the desk between them. "That's my read, but my read don't count for shit. The Guild says you're solid and they trust you, and what the Guild says goes." He scrawled a name and number on a Post-It and handed it to Win. "Name's Barton. You'll find him in Miami at that number. Wait for your assignment and then do what he tells you."

Barton, lately of Myrtle Beach, was a grizzled old man who walked funny. Win found him the day after the Miami mand-evac, and after the assignments were handed down by the Guild, and after a few false starts trying to launch into the dead zone of Biscayne Bay, Barton landed them and their supplies at a half-submerged teakwood dock adjacent to a palace that took up the entire southern end of Indian Creek Island. Their employer remained anonymous—anonymity being a foundational Guild principle—but clearly this gilt monstrosity belonged to some opulence-loving fuck knuckle whose aesthetics ran along the lines of imperial Russia. From the outside, it looked like the Winter Palace of Biscayne Bay. Inside, its meaningless excess made Win sick.

Barton assigned him to the industrial sump pumps that channeled seawater, both overland and underground, away from the property. He had gotten the hang of sumping quickly, running all the main and sublevel pumps, as well as a heavy-duty submersible that could pass solids up to three-quarters of an inch. Barton watched in silence, made a few corrections, then retreated to one of the bedrooms, where Win heard him making phone calls late at night in shattered gringo Spanish.

Three weeks in, Barton went AWOL. Win checked the usual spots they found Caretakers who had worked past their expiration dates— the rafters in the ten-car garage; the shoreline where the dead boat people sometimes got caught up in the kelp beds; the showers at the clubhouse on the abandoned golf course in the middle of the island— but Barton was gone like a blackbird and hadn't even left a note. Win called it in. He told the Guild rep he could handle the place alone; it was the company he missed.

A month later he was browsing the message boards when someone on the Submersible Avengers subgroup posted that Barton had turned up in a motel in Guadalajara dying of gangrene; his right leg had been chopped off, and it had been a sloppy job. Theories were bandied about—carbon credit laundering gone bad, drug deal double-cross, the usual. But when the truth finally came out, it was that Barton had hired a Mexican doctor to amputate his left leg because no American doctor would agree to remove a healthy limb.

2041

When the hope faded, the mourning began, but there were no rituals and neither was there solace. There was no liturgy of lament. No collective expressions of grief or penance were seen. As a result no one knew how to atone for the loss, and grief rang throughout the world. But who could atone? What were the avenues for reconciliation? How to make amends to restore this broken relationship for which no restoration was possible?

Win was not immune. The weight of it crushed him. He could not figure out how to rid himself of it. He was full Guild now and chose his own jobs. The whole thing with Barton made him feel funny. He didn't like where conversations went when Barton was brought up at Guild safehouses or on the forums. They said Barton had cracked up, that the work had turned his brain like milk gone bad, but Win had worked with him and knew he was sane. There had to have been a reason for what he'd done.

Anyway, it was easy to find postings because the East Coast was a smorgasboard of disasters and eminent domain fights and other kinds of municipal and federal heavyhandedness, so business was brisk. You could choose your hustle, and if you were good and reliable they'd fight over you. Win did a stint in Charleston when the second surge turned the Battery into a permanent reef; in Richmond when it got wet and stayed wet through the summer of '39; in Charleston again when the barrier islands finally went terminal and even the bunkers flooded when that Atlantic monster spun on a dime and turned landward and he'd had to abandon and fell out of the skiff and then had to swim up the Ashley River to avoid the Coast Guard patrols. That was the swim when he got a nasty bite from a brown water snake that mistook his right foot for a catfish; it got infected, so he saw a Guild nurse in a safe house in North Charleston; she couldn't treat the infection; she begged him to see a real doctor, and he didn't because although he couldn't quite put his finger on why, he liked the pain; it was like it was doing him a favor; some internal scale had momentarily been set right.

So he drifted south, with his swollen foot wrapped in Ace bandages and shoved into his work boot, and eventually made it down to Contadora Island, off Panama, where he took a job with a greenhorn at a tax shelter estate. By this time, the foot was black as charcoal, so swollen it was fit to burst. Win asked around, but the only medical services were on the mainland, and they were run by the military and a visit there was out of the question, unless he wanted to get out of this line of work and into the penitentiary. For a couple of days he tried to come up with options, but he kept returning to the only solution that made sense: he had to remove the foot. He wasn't concerned about losing out on work—missing fingers, toes, even the occasional foot were as common in the danger trades as scabies. Anything more, though—the other foot, a leg, an arm—and they might pull him from the terminal zones. He'd worry about that later.

Once Win settled on this course of action, he considered doing it himself, but finding the correct angle for an axe and obtaining the range of movement required to garner the force he needed to bite through bone proved impossible. The greenhorn agreed to do it for cash and booze, and Win gave him the money up front but held on to the booze for now. Steady hands were required.

A sharp hand axe found in the gardener's shed, a bottle of Tramadol leftover in the guest house bathroom, and two hesitation cuts, and it was done. As soon as the greenhorn had stopped puking, he tied it off, sanitized the wound, and, following Win's instructions, bandaged the stump. There was no pain at first, but when it came, it tried to kill him. But with it came the closest thing to peace Win had experienced since he was a child, when he and his parents had farmed the kelp and macroalgae carbon-sinks off the coast of California for the Climate Conservation Corps. Back when such efforts were meaningful and when hope was still abundant.

Two months later, a storm blew in and the main pedestal pump got gummed up by a dead rat the size of a dachshund, flooding the game room. While attempting to retrieve a partially submerged freezer, the greenhorn didn't realize the motor was still on. It fell in the water and he was electrocuted. He died instantly.

Two Guild reps arrived within the day to retrieve the body. They looked at the homemade crutches and asked Win about his missing foot, so he told them exactly what he'd done. They listened quietly, took a few notes, asked if he could see out the assignment, then left with the dead greenhorn. And although it was probably wrong, Win's concern for the boy was dwarfed by the ecstasy he'd felt—still felt, still savored, two months later—when the axe had bitten through his blackened skin, cut through the bone like it was a twig, and freed him from the offensive appendage. His heart, closed tightly as a clam, had been wrenched open, as surely as if a knife had been thrust into the capsule and twisted.

He understood now why Barton had gone to Guadalajara. The old man had been a prophet. There was a way to ease this unbearable weight he carried around. They had used up the world. They could never make things right; it was far too late for that. But a man could use himself up the way he'd helped to use up the world. Mourning wasn't enough, mourning was selfish. It was selfish because it was obsessed with the possibility of reattachment. You had to abandon this possibility; you had to actively detach. So that's what he did. This was how it began.

2049

The billionaire had requested Win's services personally, even making a preemptive laundered deposit into his bank account to sweeten the pot, and since the memory of Barton's disappearance was no longer the sour thing it had been before Win understood that the old man had given him a way forward, he'd agreed to return to the stranded asset on Biscayne Bay.

But the Winter Palace was in a terminal zone now. It was over. Miami Beach and its surrounding islands of Dr. Moreau had been called. There was no hope of future habitation here; even the floating islands—the "livable yachts"—that had been left waiting for launch were outlawed; the seas were too rough. The other billionaires had long ago emptied out their compounds and sent their plunder to former missile silos in the Black Hills. Win had to laugh. There was no counter-tech equal to the indifferent efficiency of Nature shaking off parasites.

When he'd asked the Guild rep about the job, the woman had been evasive. Finally, she admitted that the owner had asked for Win specifically. "Why me?"

"It's not my job to ask questions about why he'd want to put his assets under the protection of a gimp who cuts off his own—look, never mind. I just need to know if you'll do the job."

"Sure, why not."

"Then you need to get fit for a prosthesis for that foot."

"No."

"Those are the terms. Take it or leave it."

"Why do you care?"

"I don't. Owner wants to know you can save yourself, and some of his assets, if it comes to that. You know where you're going. You know the risks."

"Do I get a partner?"

"Yep."

"Who is it?"

"Hell if I know. Yes or no?"

There was no shortage of outlaws and grifters looking for a goose-down feather bed and three squares, but these types tapped out quickly. Sawyer was different. She was an ugly, flame-haired woman of indeterminate age with a grayish face and dark circles under her eyes. Her lips were chapped; her right eye was noticeably bigger than her left eye; and her mottled pink skin was fuzzed by fine white hairs. That first day, she and Win stood across from each other in the empty vaulted great room to go over the layout of the property, the sump pumps and basins, the solar grid, and the security system.

She surveyed the room. "Don't you think this place looks like a parallelogram had sex with a heptagon and gave birth to an encephalitic irregular polygon?" Something shifted inside him. "There are fourteen sump pumps in the compound and eight floating pumps on the grounds."

"So what? We're not here for the above-ground residence."

Win's phantom foot itched inside the prosthetic the Guild doctor had given him. "Above-ground residence?"

Sawyer stopped pulling at her hangnails. "You thought he brought you back to keep this monstrosity dry, didn't you? And look at you come running back. Limping back, I mean." She shook her head.

"I wondered why he called a guy with your specific brand of insanity, but it makes sense now. Every billionaire needs a lapdog."

She took him to the gun safe in the master bedroom. But when she opened it, Win saw it was a false door leading to an elevator. The ride down took exactly thirty seconds. Forty-five feet below the surface, it opened onto a black-granite-floored lobby with aquarium walls. The tanks were filled with vibrantly colored fish darting in circles between coral polyps and sea anenomes. "Who's been taking care of the fish?" Win asked.

"They take care of themselves," Sawyer said. She knocked on the glass. The fish did not dart away but continued their long, gliding rounds. "See? Fake, fake, fake. The finest animatronics arbitrage can buy. Come on, you ain't seen nothing yet."

He followed her across the honed black granite, his metal prosthesis clanking like a hammer striking an anvil. Then down a hallway lined with water walls and transom windows through which could be seen lush vegetation glistening with dew. He wondered if that were fake, too. The hall led into a bright three-story atrium, centrally anchored by a bamboo grove. Sunlight poured onto the plants from a skylight. "Not much of a bunker if you've got an open hole like that."

Sawyer chuckled. "It's an LED panel, dummy."

"Sorry, I've never been around stupid-rich."

"Wait until you see the bowling alley."

Win knew about the luxury apocalypse bunkers the uber-wealthy had built all over the country. He'd even invested in the life assurance sector—it exploded pre-Impact and only got bigger as the changes began unfolding with regularity. But he'd never seen anything like this one. It contained nine enormous bedrooms, an indoor pool surrounded by large windows that looked onto an underground garden bathed in simulated natural light, a medical center and a lab, a weapons room, which was adjacent to a firing range, a cavernous basketball court lined by graffiti-covered slabs of concrete boasting *pura vida* and *you really can go places with drugs* and *no police state* and other vintage New York City graffiti, a game room, and a three-story atrium filled with plants, trees, fountains, and a stone path. Sawyer

told him it had been built at the same time the above-ground residence had been built, which meant that when Win had been here
with Barton, there had been Caretakers here, living below them. He'd
never known.

He followed Sawyer across what appeared to be a steel and glass
footbridge spanning a crystal-clear stream—a breezeway, of sorts.
He looked down into the stream. There were steelhead trout holding themselves steady in the flowing water. He moved to the window.
On the other side the stream continued toward the Pacific, strange
because it was free from the haze of particulate matter. Beyond that,
the Channel Islands. "They got their geography wrong. This looks like
the California coast."

"They didn't get it wrong. It knows you're here."

"What?"

"You heard me."

Win tried to orient himself, to remind himself that he was forty-
five feet underground, that none of this was real. But then came the
smell, as fresh as if it were carried on the wind stealing through an
open window. The scent of the California coast and the mildewed life
jackets on his parents' boat and the taste of compressed air and the
wet rubber of a scuba regulator, of sugar kelp drying in the sun and
the sweat of an honest day's work. He drank in the view and the scent
like a diver taking his last breath on an empty tank.

Sawyer turned around. "You okay?"

"Smells like home. Like childhood."

"By design. He knows where you're from."

"Who the hell is he?"

"Some guy who got rich in bio-sims. Biophilic experience pods
for the obscenely wealthy. Environmental exposure therapy for the
solastalgic one-percent. He's into biologics now. Pharma. He once
asked a room full of investors if curing cancer patients was a sus-
tainable business model. He wasn't the first one to ask that question,
either. Funny how the ones who should die first always seem to live
forever."

"You have no problem taking his money."

"Neither do you."

Later, after lubricating the bearings on the pedestal sump pump in the wine cellar, Win took the elevator back to the surface and made his way across two helipads to the teakwood dock. The sun was golden-yellow, enveloped by purple clouds. Sulfate particles danced above the warm, roiling waters of the bay, a star-soaked veil. Even the dead-eyed skyscrapers of Miami spangled in the weird light like spit-polished obelisks.

Win thought about the bunker. The audacity of it. And when he thought of the audacity, he had to think of the immorality of it. The human infection, not satisfied with ruining all that grew from the earth, now burrowed into the very heart of the planet. He tried to stop the thoughts, because this was how it started, this was how the feeling overwhelmed him. But the thoughts were true. You had to look this in the eye. Looking away was wrong. Worse than wrong. It made you complicit. And so he let the feeling and the thoughts overwhelm him, because someone had to. Someone had to carry this.

Two hours later, as the elevator descended, he watched the dark droplets of blood falling onto the top of his work boot. He studied the blue and white porcelain tiles. It was a honeycombed pattern featuring honeybees. He was not revolted by the sneering irony. He was temporarily immune because of the penance he'd just performed. And though the absolution was synthetic, the respite from the shame felt good.

This thing he did was justice, drawn-out penance, but he had not yet identified its mechanism of meaning, of action. What did it accomplish, exactly? Why did it make him feel so good even as he nearly died from the pain? After all these years, the specific metaphysics of the endeavor still escaped him, which left open the possibility (he could hardly bear to entertain the idea but an honest man looked things square in the eye) that there was a luxury to his self-mutilation, and that, he had to acknowledge (looking things square), was not very different from the impulse he saw embodied all around him by a wealthy man who surrounded himself with fakes of all the things he and his psychopathic brethren had managed to erase from the world. This facsimile of an unharmed natural world was as awful as lamps made of human skin or shrunken heads on a bookshelf or necklaces made from phalangeal bones. It was evil.

His heart thumped. It seemed like the first time in a very long time that he'd felt it beat. Down, down the elevator went. Despite the makeshift tourniquet he had tied around his wrist, there was a pretty good pool of blood spreading over the porcelain honeybees. He looked at the pulp of his mutilated joint and the gibbous moons of his neatly severed radius and ulna. The pain was monstrous; it was like a living thing that fed itself on each ragged breath he took. The edges of his vision flickered. It seemed the elevator was destined for the burning liquid heart of the planet.

Later, he awoke in a bed, tucked in as neatly as a doll. All the windows were curtained but one, through which poured a smoky twilight that looked engineered but felt deeply familiar. Sawyer sat on a chair, the metal prosthesis on her lap. She watched him with her rheumy eyes as she finished off a bag of dried chickpeas. "Welcome back." When she said these two words in her frog-like voice, Win felt that thing move in him again.

"Morning," he said. "The pumps working?"

"Plain sailing."

Win sat up and reached over to turn on his bedside lamp, but instead of a hand, a white-wrapped capsule emerged from beneath the bedclothes. "Did you do this?"

Sawyer shook the last of the Chex mix into her hand. "Nope. You did. I just cleaned it up."

"I meant the bandaging. It's professional."

"I know what you meant. You made a mess and were no help since you had passed out. I did what I had to do. If this is your thing, you should be better at it." She crumpled up the empty bag and dropped it on the floor. "She told me about you, but I didn't believe her. That people did this. Cut off their own body parts. But apparently it's a thing. Apotemnophilia. I looked it up. It's when—"

"I know what it is. That's not what I have. That's mental illness."

"And what do you call this, Doc?"

"This is a freely chosen action. An offering. An apology."

"You don't strike me as a penitent."

"Then you don't know me."

She walked over to the bed. Her cheeks were livid, the lines in her forehead as deep as faults. Her salt-dusted lips were peeling. "You have the sickness, you know."

"What sickness?"

"This thing that's out there. This disease. Where the Changes make you sick."

"Wrong. Sickness happens to you. I made this happen. Sympathetic deconstruction. It is the sanest thing I've ever done. I choose to do this. I am not sick."

"Suicide in slow motion. Have you asked even yourself how you will continue this sympathetic deconstruction when you have no hands? When you've taken your last leg?"

"Yes. You'll help me."

"I see. You want me for your surgeon-valet. Help break you down until you're just a bundle of clothes on the floor?"

"Admit that what I do makes sense."

"Even if I did, what makes you think I have the stomach to help you mutilate yourself?"

"You can stomach caretaking the spoils of a billionaire. My militant pilgrimage isn't the problem. It's not a sickness to be cured." She looked at him. The key had stopped spinning in the lock. Win saw that it had caught. "I know you want to help me. That's why you're here. He sent you into the heart of darkness to find out what's going on with Kurtz."

"You think a guy like him, with his resources, didn't already know? He knew about what Barton had done in Guadalajara before you did."

"How?"

"How the hell should I know? Late-stage capitalists always find a meal. The boss wants to put you in a drug trial. He thinks you have the sickness. That you can be cured with this drug. He thinks if someone like you can be cured then everyone can."

"Heh."

"What?"

"A cure? Cure for what? Regret? There's no cure for that except putting the world back together."

Sawyer laid her hand on the bed, close to but not touching Win's bandaged hand. He felt the phantom move inside him again. "So what's the plan, then? The arm next?" she asked. Win nodded. "Can I ask you a question? Just so I've got this thing straight in my mind?"

"Go ahead."

"Why did you go to the trouble to eliminate the hand if you knew you were just going to take the arm off later?"

"Didn't the reef die before the ocean boiled?"

The false wind outside sucked the curtains against the screens in the windows that looked out onto a false scene, held them there, then released them, and on the release Win felt something inside him let go, too. It had let go in order to make room for her. The phantom sat on his heart as Win looked at her; it had no face but he knew its name.

2050

The wind from the chopper's rotors hashed the salty air and made the silver oxeye that had grown up through the cracks in the dilapidated helicopter pad bow like dancers at curtain's close. Win sat on the edge of the pad in the makeshift wheelchair Sawyer had made for him out of a dining room chair and a wheeled pallet after she'd removed his right leg. He watched as the billionaire's hired EMTs conferred. The need for justice was not yet appeased, but neither was this feeling for her. This need. And though for months she'd betrayed nothing more than a vague affection, and as they, together, took him apart piece by piece and approached his terminal dismantling, she changed. The way her eyes looked at his face. The occasional softness in her voice. Her rare smiles.

Then one day she wheeled him out to the end of the teakwood dock so they could watch the sunset and told him she was done. She wouldn't finish him off. If he didn't enroll in the trial, if he didn't at least give the drug a chance, she'd leave. There were plenty of billionaires who needed her expert services, and she had no problem taking their money.

As Win followed the lugubrious movements of a faraway Strato-tanker he understood for the first time the cupidity of love. It wanted everything and it would do anything to get it. She still thought he was sick. He knew he was saner than everyone else. But the end of the world was nothing to the idea of her absence, and so Win agreed to cure his conscience with drugs.

They loaded him onto the chopper and strapped him in. It rose into the air like a bird. When it cut back toward Miami, he saw her standing on the end of the dock, her wild hair flying about her head, and thought about the days when his only fear was that he would die only half-redeemed as the world fell apart around him.

YOUR GHOST REMAINS UPRIGHT

(Deacon Kompkoff-Blackwood)

Deacon Kompkoff-Blackwood

Ely, Minnesota

Diagnosis: DSM-7, 650.9: Environmental Illness, Solastalgia
[Environmental Hyperempathy, Tree]

2035

He was fifteen when it started, the year he broke. Later, Deacon understood that this was how they'd gotten in. They got in through the broken places. It had been early June when Deacon's mother began work on the gypsy moth mating disruption program over in Cook County. A DNR forester assigned to the critically endangered Laurentian Mixed Forest Province outside of Ely, her game was insect infestations. Billions of trees had already been defoliated by the insatiable moth larvae, with billions more projected to die. It rarely got cold enough in the winters anymore to kill off the moth larvae. This mass death was an integral part of the evolutionary machinery the trees relied on to survive, she told Deacon. Now the infestations came in six-year cycles and there was almost no time for the trees to recover. Then that spring, official confirmation came from the university silviculturists in the Cities: the cycles were now three years.

Of course, Deacon's mother and the other forestry workers already knew that, but confirmation meant state money, maybe even federal. Deacon had gone down with her to one of the state forests south of Ely—he couldn't remember which—to help broadcast-apply female moth pheromone. By some sexual alchemy, this pheromone prevented the worst of the infestations.

The things happening in forestry were weird. A decade earlier, groups of Alaskan white spruce—explorers, his mother called them— had started venturing north into parts of the Arctic they'd never been before, somehow hopping over mountains and rooting in the tundra. The trees moved quickly, more quickly than expected. It was as if they were walking. As if they were sentient. That's how she spoke of them, and one time, because he'd been scolded in school the week before for anthropomorphizing ants during a science presentation, Deacon scolded her. "Don't do that. Don't make them seem like, alive, with feelings and stuff."

"You don't think trees are living creatures?"

"Obviously I know they're alive, but they're not alive like us. Everyone knows that."

"How is the way we're alive different from the way trees are alive?" This was a question that seemed to have an obvious answer, but it eluded Deacon.

"We just are," he said lamely.

"Did you know that trees scream?"

"Mom."

"All I'm saying is that they're living creatures and they're suffering. We need to listen to them."

Deacon's heart immediately closed up shop. He hated when she did this. There was too much suffering to keep track of. Acknowledging the pain of trees trying to survive a cataclysmic climatic shift? Imagining them screaming for his attention? No, it was too much to ask. He couldn't acknowledge it all, because if he acknowledged it all then he would have to carry it all, and he couldn't. No one could.

IT WAS THE SECOND NIGHT of the gypsy moth operation, after the long drive back to Ely, when it happened. They were eating a couple of vending machine sandwiches as they stood at the kitchen counter. She'd been laughing as Deacon told the story about Ben-o and the girl he liked and how the girl had kissed another boy named Ben at a party, and she'd said something funny like, "Maybe she can't help it. Maybe she just has a thing for boys named Ben," but the end of the sentence came out sounding garbled. The sandwich fell from her hand. Her face had gone slack. Her right eye was open and bright, the left was droopy and sad. Her mouth hung open, as if she were astonished. She limped past him into the living room and lay down on the old couch. Deacon knelt next to her while she stared at the ceiling and waited. Eventually, she lifted her right arm and pointed at the sudoku book on the coffee table, with a Bic serving as bookmark. Deacon handed it to her and she wrote a word across the top of Puzzle #101.

Hospital.

THE SCANS SHOWED that the stroke had been massive. The doctor asked Deacon if he knew whether she had a patent foramen ovale. "A small hole in the heart," he added. "She would have been born with it. Blood clots can slip through and travel to the brain, causing strokes."

Across the room she lay still and pale as frost, her eyes closed and a tube drilled into her throat.

The nurses brought Deacon blankets and granola bars while he waited for his father to come up from Biwabik. One of them squeezed his shoulder and said, "There's nothing you can do. They have to want to live."

Eventually, Deacon's father showed up to sign the papers that needed signing. In the lobby he complained that they couldn't be signed electronically and then asked Deacon for gas money for the return trip. He didn't even go in to look at her.

But Deacon did. He looked at her and wondered all the usual things, like where she was and if she could hear him. He wondered if the bright spots on the scans the doctor had shown him were empty, peaceful spaces or if they were scars from an infestation. Maybe her mind had been defoliated. Maybe trees did scream even though you couldn't hear them. Maybe she did, too.

GRIEF IS AS COMMON as small deceptions and as blinding as the January sun. It didn't turn everything black, the way singers said; if it did, that would have made it harder for Deacon to see the contours of his pain, which would have been good comfort. Instead, it emanated cold and unrelenting light that revealed every little thing, the shame and regret and the rocky wastes of the days ahead he was now expected to live through, alone.

He quit his job at Casey's and closed up the house, gave the cats to a neighbor, and hitchhiked south, past Embarrass and Aurora to the Mesabi Trail outside Biwabik. As he walked the three miles to his father's trailer, he wondered what the kids at Mesabi East were like. Considering the school pulled from Hoyt Lakes, Embarrass, Aurora, and every little town in between, he figured he wouldn't be the only kid who slept on a couch in a double-wide.

He could hear Penny barking at squirrels before the trailer came into sight. His dog. His good old girl. When he was six, he'd found her in an old laundry bag behind the Pillow Rocks monument north of town, the only one of six puppies still alive. She was tiny, the runt. He'd put her in a towel-lined shoebox and nursed her back to health in front of the wood-burning stove. She had the dark eyes and muzzle of a German shepherd and the floppy ears of a golden retriever.

His father called her Vixen, tried to train her as a guard dog, but the mutt was too dumb for such things. Too much golden, his father often said with disgust. He lost interest in the dog, and Deacon began calling her Penny. Lucky Penny. When Deacon was ten and his father left them for Lisa, he took Penny with him to Biwabik, because Lisa liked dogs.

As soon as Penny saw Deacon walking up the gravel driveway from the road, she let loose a full-throated wail and raced toward him, but she was staked and when she reached the end of her chain she flew backward. She did it again and again until Deacon unhooked her and buried his face in her fur. His father stood at the screen door. Deacon walked up the steps to the trailer, but his father didn't step aside to let him pass.

"Was there any money?" Deacon shrugged; he didn't know anything about that. His father cursed and looked back over his shoulder at Lisa, who lay sprawled on the couch, heavily pregnant. "Wait here." He shut the door in Deacon's face.

Deacon sat down on the step to think. Penny forced her muzzle under his arm and whined, and Deacon pulled her close. A couple of minutes later, the door opened and his father stood there with an envelope in his hand. "You can't stay here. Try her people. She probably has people somewhere."

Deacon stood to leave, and his father handed him the envelope. "Should be enough to get back to Ely, then some. You're lucky your stepmom has a heart. You tell that lawyer where he can find me. I'm right here, and I know what's comin' to me."

"I'm taking Penny."

"That's Lisa's dog now. Go on and put her back on the line before you leave." He went back inside without saying goodbye.

Deacon walked down the gravel driveway until he got to the hard-top of Mesabi Trail. He walked about a mile and didn't turn around once. He waited until he got to where Vermillion Trail crossed Mesabi before turning around to check. Nothing. His heart sank. Then an old F150 came rumbling down the road from the direction of town and the driver flagged him down. Penny was in the bed. When the truck stopped, she leapt out and jumped up on Deacon.

"I was gonna ask if this here was your dog, but I guess I already know. Didn't want her to get hit so I picked her up. You got a leash?"

Penny helped land rides. They got as far as Tower in a matter of hours. It was near sunset when the driver let them off in front of the Presbyterian church on the corner of Spruce and 2nd. Deacon decided against trying to hitch the last leg to Ely, even though he was only twenty miles outside town, because he was too tired to chat, and the people always wanted to chat.

So and Penny made their way down the Voyageur highway, crossed over at the place where the speed limit changed from 35 to 50 mph, and scrambled down the banks of the East Two River. Penny chased invisible creatures in the leaf litter, pouncing and freezing, astonished when Deacon would kick the leaves away and there would be nothing there.

They went deeper into the forest, over coarse, loamy till and scarred bedrock. This, like nearly all the forests up here, was part of the Laurentian Mixed Forest Province, glacier-scoured and stark, but also brimming with greens and yellows in places. It had once been lush with red and white pine, paper birch, balsam, and spruce, a fact Deacon knew from learning and books, and from her, rather than from experience. While there were thin groves of jack pines growing on droughty ridges and bedrock, and aspen and birch still took root here, the red and white pine were long gone, clear-cut in the nineteenth and twentieth centuries. You had to look hard to find quaking aspen, even harder to find the tamarack, the larch that burst into gold, bright as a Roman candle.

Eventually, Deacon found a family of tamaracks with a smooth patch of ground between them. He kicked away the carpet of fallen needles and laid out his bedroll. He had a bowl in his backpack that he'd brought from home and he went to the river and filled it with water for Penny, but she walked into the river right up to her belly and drank her fill. They returned to their camp under the trees and he gave her a bite of his sandwich. Then she curled up, sighed deeply, and fell asleep at his feet.

Deacon finished the sandwich and drank some water, then pulled out his Device, but it was dead so he lay down, with his backpack under his head. The sun was still above the horizon, but the understory was already twilit. It was warm and the frogs' songs were hearty as sea shanties. Deacon thought about what he was going to do next. He didn't want to go home. He didn't want to go to school. Maybe he'd end up in foster care. Probably, he would. Maybe instead of hitching back to Ely tomorrow, he'd head south, toward the Cities, where he and Penny could disappear for a while.

Then it was time to close his eyes and let the grief come for him.

It was so big; it was everywhere and it was in everything. As Deacon lay under the larches, he let the grief colonize him. It insisted, and he accepted its insistence, that it had always been part of the world, that it was not a pathology but was instead ingrained in existence, whether a human, a bird, or a tree. For the first time, he felt the voices of the trees around him. They did not scream. Instead, they murmured like a restless crowd awaiting the opening of a curtain. Certain voices rose above the others and addressed him directly. Pleading voices, of different timbres. Voices filled with sorrow. Words that were not words. *Touch me,* one sobbed. Another begged, *Tell me it will be okay.* Others complained of sickness. Many queried after lost family members. Sentience was all around him, even in the stillest things. It sought a way in, even though human beings were closed vessels. Closed, except in grief, because grief broke us apart, and if you were in the right place at the right time when you were broken, you could become part of the world. You could hear all the voices. You could let it in.

The trees clamored for his attention because they had finally found him.

THE SICKNESS

(Santiago Faucheaux)

Santiago Faucheaux

New Orleans, Louisiana

Diagnosis: DSM-7, 650.4: Environmental Illness, Solastalgia
[Natural Disaster Dissociative Disorder]

2036

Santi had first seen Jude at lice check the summer he went to Camp Mowaskin. They sat in chairs directly facing one another in the dining hall as nurses wearing surgical gloves performed their task like bored phrenologists. Jude stared at him with his dark, hooded eyes while his head was pulled this way and that. Afterward, they carried their duffels to their assigned cabins.

"You're the scholarship kid," Jude said as they walked. "The one from New Orleans. Your folks can't pay for camp so the camp pays for you to come." Jude recited these facts like they were a series of criminal charges. "Don't worry," Jude continued. "Everybody knows, but it's no big deal. Nobody else here's poor, though, except Weston. He's from Florida. But he's on the Atheist Reclamation Scholarship and is only here because he doesn't believe the Changes are God's plan. He doesn't believe in God, even." Jude shook his head sadly. "Can you imagine not believing in God when God believes in you? What's your name?"

"Santiago."

"Kind of dumb name is that?"

"You can call me Santi."

"That doesn't make it any better. I'm Jude."

"Are you in my cabin?"

"What cabin are you in?"

Santi lifted the badge that had been placed around his neck at check-in. "Job's Lament?"

Jude chuckled. "That's the haunted one. I'm in Ezekiel's Bones— used to be Loon Lodge."

"Is that close to Job's Lament?"

"Yeah, don't worry, it's next door."

"I wasn't worried."

Jude smirked. "Okay, champ."

At Mowaskin, the trees rose up around the camp strong and healthy, and bursting with so many emerald green leaves that it seemed impossible that even one more could unfold. Under the canopy the air was cool and sweet, as different from the suffocating heat of home as the weird accents of the other campers. All day long, Santi heard birdsong—from curious chirps to sorrowful cries to the keening wail of raptors. At night, loons laughed on the lake. These were sounds he'd only heard on his phone when he streamed "Nature Nighttime." And swimming was allowed at Mowaskin because the water was safe, not yet warm enough to be infested by the brain-eating amoebas that had ruined the lakes back home.

That first afternoon, the campers were summoned to a small amphitheater on the shore of the lake. Weathered signposts lining the wood-chipped path bore messages like *Welcome the Changes* and *God Controls the Climate* and *Why Worry?* As the boys noisily filed in to take their seats on the wooden benches, the counselors stood shoulder to shoulder on the stage. They were dressed in black and had their hands clasped behind their backs.

Pastor Will held a gnarled tree branch in his hand. One by one, he called the boys to the front and asked them, "What is Impact?" Each boy recited the same line, as if he'd been born with it on his lips: "There is no Impact, but His impact; there is no change, but His Change." Jude nudged Santi with his elbow as a boy stepped over the benches on his way to the front of the amphitheater. "That's Weston," he said. "This oughta be good."

"What is Impact, son?" Pastor Will asked.

Weston smirked at the boys in the audience. "Impact is the direct result of preventable climate change caused by man." Pastor Will brought the tree branch down on Weston's shoulders with a sickening crack. Weston cried out and fell to his knees. Clutching his shoulder, he scrambled to his feet and backed away from the pastor.

"You got that one wrong, son. There is no Impact but His impact. No Change but His change. As it pleases God to replenish the lakes and rivers with rain, so it pleases Him to withhold that sustenance at His pleasure. If the heaven over our heads shall be bronze and the earth under our feet shall be iron and the Lord God make the rain of our land powder and dust, then this is the Plan. We welcome the Changes in His name."

Weston wiped his eyes with his sleeve and looked up at Pastor Will. "Nothing you can say will change the fact that it's real, what's happening. And people did it—not some spirit in the sky."

"Just shut up," Jude muttered under his breath.

The pastor considered the tree branch in his hands. He seemed surprised when he realized Weston had stopped talking. "Go ahead. Say your piece, son."

Santi could tell that Weston sensed the trap, but it seemed so important to him, what he was saying, that he persisted. "The thing you call the Sickness is real. It's a real disease." Weston looked into the heart of the amphitheater, appealing for an ally. Finding none, the boy turned back to the pastor. "It's why our parents sent us here. They think you can fix us, but you can't. It's the Changes. That's what's making us sick." He thrust out his arms toward Pastor Will, as if asking for an embrace, but instead he was displaying innumerable white scars on his brown skin: horizontal lines, vertical lines, some thick, some whisper-thin. "I have it!"

As Pastor Will turned the tree limb in his hands, he asked the boys, "Who cares about this boy's soul?" Jude joined the other campers in raising his arm high, and when he saw Santi kept his down, he gripped his wrist and jerked it up. "Who cares enough about his soul to help cure him of his arrogance? To help him release this evil delusion and accept that sickness comes not from external causes but from within, that it comes from his unwillingness to accept and rejoice in the Plan, which unfolds all around us as promised, glory to God?" The boys' arms remained raised. They couldn't very well lower them now, Santi thought. "Who will help this child of God understand what is obvious to those who cherish Christ and His promise of return, that this planet was never meant to be our permanent home? That we were commanded to use it."

Pastor Will's voice grew louder now. "This earth is disposable because our souls are not! These changes prepare the way for the righteous to take their place in heaven. This sickness is Satan's last gasp as he fights his annihilation!" Santi was startled to see tears streaming down the faces of the counselors who stood off to the side. Pastor Will reached over and took hold of Weston's arm and held it high above his head. "Who cares about this boy?" he thundered.

At the very end of the second row, a boy stood up. "Mr. Van Dyke cares," Pastor Will said. "Come, Peter." Santi watched as the boy walked toward the stage. His shoulders were straight, his chin was up. He kept his eyes fixed on the wooden cross as he walked. Santi had never seen a boy with such purpose in his body, like a man wielding a hammer. Pastor Will placed the thick branch in Peter's hand. The counselors took hold of Weston's arms and turned him roughly so he was facing the lake. "Save him!" Santi wrenched around in his seat to see where the shouted encouragement had come from and saw several boys on their feet, their eyes wild with excitement. Peter raised the branch high above his head and brought it down on Weston's back. Weston's knees buckled and the counselors jerked him up. Peter struck him again. More cries came from the other side of the amphi-

theater where other boys had leapt to their feet. "No Impact but His!"
"Accept the Plan!" "Save him!" "Cast the devil out!" Next to him, Jude
prayed silently, his hands clasped in his lap. Santi covered his eyes.
Weston's screams echoed across the lake, but the sound of the dead
wood striking his body remained trapped in the amphitheater.

SANTI WAS SIX the first time he disappeared from the FEMA camp
outside Lakeview, where he lived with his mother after his father left
for work in the Arizona water mines. He was found later that day at
the Tchefuncte River Lighthouse picking through a shell midden and
not answering to his name. The cops guessed he'd walked the whole
six miles from the trailer park in his bare feet. He matched the photo
so they put him in the back of the cruiser and brought him home.

For six days, he did not respond to his name, not even when Pastor
Souweine came and sat on the sofa bed, fingering the leopard-print
throw and intoning, *Oh self-existent eternal Jehovah, please intercede
for this child who is a prisoner to this disability—we speak your promise over our brother that those who the mighty tyrant has kidnapped
shall be rescued.* Then the pastor showed him some card tricks, even
gave him a deck of cards to play with, but made him promise never
to gamble. His mother sent him out to play in the gravel and dust so
she could speak to the pastor alone, and when Santi came back in
to show the pastor how he'd figured out how to fan the cards like a
magician, he found them with their bodies pressed together, their
lips touching, and the pastor's hand pressed between his mother's
legs. He was too young to make sense of the longing he felt for the
world to open up and swallow him whole. At six it was just a sadness
he didn't understand.

Three years later he disappeared at recess and was found on the
Causeway, standing in the middle of a group of birdwatchers who had
come hoping to see the purple martins who once swarmed the south
end of the bridge before sailing under the bridge to roost. The birds
had not been seen in four years, but still the people came. Santi told
the cops his name was TJ, but they remembered about him and held
him until Pastor Souweine, who was now his stepdaddy, got to the

crossover where the birding group had gathered. They drove directly to the church, because once was a fluke but twice was God. The congregants laid hands on him. He had caught the Holy Spirit. He couldn't say when he slipped back into himself, but it almost seemed beside the point, since all it meant was that God had gently returned him to the mortal plane.

At twelve, he disappeared for four days during the June crawfish molt and was on the news. He was described as being five-foot-two with sandy blond hair, blue eyes, wearing an orange windbreaker and waders and carrying a trap. On the fifth day, he was pulled from Lake Pontchartrain by two deckhands, half-naked and facedown but somehow alive. At the hospital, the doctors asked him how long he'd been in the lake; he told them the truth, which was that he had never left the lake, that he had always been in the lake. They had laid out his belongings on the table on wheels and someone had kindly taken out all the cards from the deck and laid them out to dry, even though they were unsalvageable. One of the nurses brought him a new deck and he showed her his best tricks.

He did not know his mother when she arrived from work, so it seemed to him that the doctors were telling his business to a tired old woman. They told her where he'd been found, that his skin showed signs of prolonged immersion, that his knees were scraped up as if by rocks, and his back was sunburnt. They felt he'd probably been in the lake all night. She was too tired to care. She listened in silence. Based on his prior disappearances, and in consultation with the pediatric psychiatrist on staff, they suspected some kind of dissociative disorder. Serial fugue states. A psychiatric workup was recommended. The pastor was gone by now, living on a houseboat on Ruddock Canal with a deckhand's widow, so there was no one to say that he was touched by the Lord God and therefore could not and should not be touched by shrinks, who were Satan's pipe fitters. But she was too tired.

When the federal housing subsidies were finally disbursed, the Lakeview FEMA camp closed down. Of course, the people in the camp didn't receive the cash themselves—poor folk could not be trusted with such sums. Instead, the money went through bureaucratic intermediaries and came out the other end as Section 8 housing well outside the five-hundred-year flood plains. Santi and his mother moved into an efficiency apartment in an old motel called the Riverview, built atop Ozark fieldstones.

By this time, Santi knew he was not touched. He knew he was mentally ill. He had read online all about fugues, knew that their causes were mysterious, that they lay at the edge of knowledge, knew he was hardly alone in them. He found stories of kids and old people, all exhibiting strange behavior. There was a girl out near Plaquemines who'd lost her house in the surge, got a new house from Habitat for Humanity, then later couldn't stop dancing. Danced until her feet were bloody. Her mom said she cried the whole time. And the old people, they got it, too. Just look in any trailer in Lakeview. *Solastalgia,* they called it. There was talk that this was all because of the Changes, but no one wanted to talk about that.

After Pastor Souweine ran off, they joined a new church. The congregation was small but fervent, and they didn't think like the pastor did about the fugues. God would not lead a young boy to nearly drowning himself in Pontchartrain. Satan would, though. That's exactly what he would do. Must be that Santi was following Satan sure as the children followed the rat catcher of Hamelin. Only God could heal. The church took up a collection to send Santi to the conversion camp up north and came up with half the fee. Mowaskin picked up the rest. In the scholarship letter, Pastor Will had written, "We can't wait to watch God move as He helps us snatch this boy's troubled soul out of Satan's hand."

On the train to Minnesota, Santi sat next to a man on his way to St. Paul, who spent hours scrolling through funny pictures of tough-looking dogs with unexpected names—a pit bull named Chad, a mastiff called James, a German Shephard named Eleanor—and videos of the improbable and the fake. He showed Santi a clip that looked like a polar bear steering a large ship. "Deepfake, but funny, right?" the man said.

Santi pulled one of his decks from his traveling bag and showed the man the Sybil Cut, splitting the deck into multiple sections, then lifting and layering each section atop one another using only one hand, and tried to teach him how to do it. He let Santi use his phone while he tried to replicate the cut. That way neither of them had to look out the windows.

A FEW DAYS INTO SANTI'S STAY at Mowaskin, the temperature climbed to the high nineties. The loons no longer cried at night and the bird-song had disappeared. Back home in Louisiana, the heat was heavy, wet, swampy. Here, the air felt brittle enough to break. The heat made it hard to sleep. One of the boys in his cabin had night terrors and had to sleep with restraints; his thrashing and unpredictable screams kept Santi awake. Worse, the desire to be swallowed up and spit out somewhere else, as someone else, was growing strong again. He told Jude about the boy with the night terrors and Jude told him to wait until lights out, sneak out of Job's Lament with his sleeping bag, sneak into Bones, and share his bunk. It was easy: Counselor Finn was always the first one asleep in Job's Lament and Counselor Dave slept with earplugs, even though he wasn't supposed to. Santi knew how to wake before sunrise to sneak back to his bunk. Jude skipped canoeing to join Santi in Arts & Crafts, where they painted banners featuring Pastor Will's best-known sayings, like, *This earth is disposable because our souls are not!* and *No Impact But His.*

One day, in the communal showers, Jude told Santi that he could jerk off without detection if he just made it look like he was just soaping up real good. The scales fell from Santi's eyes; he'd wondered why all the boys in the shower had been so scrupulous about their nether regions. "I thought that was illegal here."

Jude tilted his head back to rinse the shampoo from his hair. "It's a loophole. They can't tell you not to jerk off because the Bible doesn't even mention it. No one knows what God thinks about whacking off. I mean, honestly, if you think about it, He actually invented it, right? Anyway, the only thing is that you can't think about random girls or their tits or anything."

"What are you supposed to think about, then?"

"Your future wife, obviously."

"That's a random woman."

"Stop thinking so much." He bent his head under the stream of water so it ran down his body in rivulets. Santi felt a stirring, like grains of sand dancing in his bloodstream. When Jude noticed he was still standing there, he flicked water at him. "Take a picture, why don't you? That way you can jack off to me whenever you want." Santi forced a laugh and said, "You wish."

At supper, Jude and Santi sat together. One night, when after they ate franks and beans and lime Jell-O, and everyone had bussed their trays, the associate pastor, Pastor Bob, got up from his seat and sauntered up to the rolling podium next to the upright piano. Unlike Pastor Will, Pastor Bob was young and had a cool haircut. He also had a light ministerial touch and let a lot of things slide, like mild cursing and horseplay in the showers. He was the one Santi talked to during individual therapy. Now, he leaned on the podium surveying the noisy room. "I can wait all night, guys," he said, smiling. Amid a chorus of shushes, the room quieted down. He let the silence sit for a moment. "Hear that? That's the sound of an open line to God. I hear kids tell me, 'Oh, Pastor Bob, God is so much louder when I'm here.'" He shook his head. "God's not louder. The world is quieter here." He glanced down at the podium and grinned. "Look at me—looking like a teacher. It's summer! Illegal to even think about school, right?"

He pushed the podium away and walked over to where Santi was sitting. "What does it mean to be sick, Santiago?"

"I guess it depends on what kind of sick you mean."

He laughed. "Good answer. What does it mean to be spiritually sick?"

"To be separated from the Lord."

"Good. Do you think you're spiritually sick?" Santi reddened. This was the same question Pastor Bob had asked him earlier that day during their session. He knew it would be unwise to answer in front of Pastor Will how he'd answered Pastor Bob. But of course it was also impossible to lie. He felt the eyes of the entire mess hall on him. "Go ahead, Santi."

"No."

"That's not what you told me earlier today. Earlier today you said you were sick."

"I mean that I'm not spiritually sick. I am not separated from God. But I am sick, I just don't think God's making me sick. I don't think he would do that. Especially to a kid."

"Would it surprise you to know that I agree with you?" A vibration passed from table to table. "Because I do agree with you," he said mildly. "God isn't making you sick. Satan is. The thing they call the Sickness is Satan's lie, designed to prevent the preparations for the promised coming of Christ. Now I want to show you something."

Counselor Dave picked up a cardboard box and handed it to the pastor, who pulled out a pill bottle and held it up like it was an artifact from a dead era. "So many of you boys came here with these kinds of bottles, all of 'em full of little lies pressed into tablets and shot into capsules. You swallow these little lies every single day with a glass of water and you believe they can make you well. But you cannot medicate Satan away. He grows stronger on the lies because he feeds on them!"

Murmurs rose up among the boys. Counselor Dave picked up a waste bin and carried it over to where Pastor Bob was peering at the bottle's label. "Sal Murietta?" A pale hand shot up at a table near the door. "These lies belong to you. Do you want to keep feeding Satan?"

"No!" a small voice called back, and the boys cheered. Pastor Bob emptied the pills into the trash. He picked another bottle from the box and called another boy's name, asking if he wanted to keep swallowing lies. No one wanted to help Satan. This went on until every bottle had been emptied. Counselor Dave swept the bottles back into the cardboard box and whisked away the waste bin.

"And now we pray," Pastor Bob said. "Let us give thanks for the fires of righteousness, for the rising seas. Let us give thanks for the wayward flocks that roost in unfamiliar places and for the great glaciers that become streams. These are the signs of God's promised return and the beginning of our everlasting reward."

Santi heard Jude weeping and opened his eyes. All around him, boys were weeping, crying as if their hearts would break.

No "ELECTRONICS" were allowed at Mowaskin, so a deck of cards was a marvel and a budding cardist a magician. Santi was working his way through a long list of boys who wanted to be tutored, but he reserved the hour between devotions and lights out for Jude, when the counselors were in the evening meeting and the boys could speak freely.

"Pastor Will's right," Jude said one night, as Santi was helping him learn how to do a one-hand cut.

"Right about what?"

"The Changes. How God is pulling the strings. What's happening down south is just his way of saying 'Hey, what's up, dweebs? Judgment Day, it's a-comin', I'm still all-knowing, still able to get shit done, so pay attention.'" He stretched his fingers around the deck and tried in vain to use his thumb to split it. "This shit is impossible, man."

Santi grinned. He liked the way Jude chewed on his lip when he tried to replicate one of the card tricks, and he liked how he could sometimes catch Jude looking at him and not the cards. He took the deck from Jude's hands and cleanly split it. He turned it over in his hand so Jude could see. "Use your middle finger to push the lower half of the deck. The two halves have to be basically perpendicular." He handed back the deck. Jude's dark hair fell in his eyes and his mouth fell open as he struggled to get the two halves into position.

"You know what they say about Judgment Day, right?" Santi said. "It'll be awful."

"Yeah, but it'll be worth it. We'll be taken up to Heaven. Who cares."

For the hundredth time, Santi wondered why Jude was at Mowaskin—what was so wrong with him that he ended up here? Some of the boys you could tell right off, like the boy with the night terrors and the kid who thought his body was infested by bugs. Others were just withdrawn or quiet or prone to unexpected fits of rage or weeping. And then there were boys like Jude, who seemed perfectly fine. Santi knew asking was not allowed because by asking you insinuated that the Sickness was real, but he couldn't bear it any longer. "What's your sickness?" A couple of boys glanced their way.

Jude shook his head and stared at the deck in his hands. "You know you're not supposed to ask that."

"Why not?" Santi asked, even though he knew. He just wanted to hear Jude say it.

"Because—" He peeked at Santi through his bangs. "Because— *theoretically*—we're not sick. The Sickness is a hoax. It's a lie made up by people who want any excuse to take over the world. Think about it: if they say that the Changes are making us sick, then they can, like, have an excuse to take over entire countries and government and stuff."

"Who are 'they?'"

"It's not like I've got a list of names. Powerful people. Like government people and rich people. They made this up. They want to make it into an epidemic so they can force medicine down our throats, subdue us, turn us into sheep. My dad said it's just a total power grab."

"I thought it was because we didn't accept 'the plan.'"

"How are you so dumb? It's both. Like, it's all mixed up with the government not letting kids pray in schools. They're trying to separate us from God because they know we get sick if we are, and being sick makes us weak, and if we're weak then we can be dominated and we can't prepare the way for Christ's return. Come on. We're here because we need to strengthen our belief in the plan. The Sickness is not real." Jude still struggled with the deck, so Santi took it from his hands once again, set one half on the mattress between them and handed the other half back.

"Try it with half a deck first. It's easier." He watched Jude work the half-deck for a while, then decided to say it. "Well, the sickness is real."

Jude's eyes shot up. "What did you say?"

"You heard me. It's real. Look how much worse some of the boys are since Pastor Bob threw away their pills."

"They're just weak. Satan can dominate them."

"Well, I know I'm sick. I up and disappear. Forget who I am. Don't know how I end up where I end up. Sometimes I remember my name right away. Sometimes it takes weeks for me to get back home. Once it took three months. I black out. I go places. Can't remember my mom. Where I come from it's called the Fugue, but it has a real name. It's in the books."

Other boys in the cabin were watching Santi now. No one spoke. The floor fans hummed like insects. "Dissociative disorder." The voice came from the bunk above where Santi and Jude sat. "Amnesia. Alternative identities. The traveling fugue."

"Leave it to Weston," someone said.

Santi knocked his knuckles against the slats of the upper bunk. "Hey, how did you know that?"

"Ow, don't rock the bed." Weston had returned from his therapy session with Pastor Will that afternoon, limping, and hadn't been at supper. Weston's hand appeared from the upper bunk. He was holding a phone. The room buzzed. A smuggled Device! Weston's stock went up immediately. "Here," he said. "It's all here. Every last one of you sickos—you're all here." Santi took the phone. It was open to a spreadsheet containing an alphabetical list of the campers, followed by numbers and terms Santi had never seen before.

"What is all this?"

"The diagnoses," Weston replied. "What everybody's here for."

"We're here to know God," a boy said timidly.

"Terry, come on," Weston said. "I've been reading through it since yesterday, looked everything up. You're not here to know God. You're here because you're fucked up in the head."

"How did you get this, Weston?" Santi asked.

"The database password was JesusSaves316. They're morons. I got in on, like, the second try." Santi barely heard him. He scrolled up and down the spreadsheet, looking for Jude's name. The boys pressed close to the bunk. "Read it out loud!"

"Don't." Santi looked over at Jude and saw a look on his face he'd never seen before. Fear. But not the kind of fear Santi had grown used to seeing here, not fear of punishment or pain, but fear of being found out. He'd seen it on Pastor Souweine's face that time he'd walked into the bedroom and found the man folding up the collection dollars, securing them with rubber bands, then shoving them into his pockets.

There were howls of protest over the delay. Santi met Jude's eye and nodded his head very slightly. Jude relaxed. "Yeah, come on, read it!"

"Do Thorpe!" someone shouted.

"Harry Thorpe: Cotard Delusion."

"What the heck is that?"

"Walking corpse disease," Weston said from his bunk. "Thinks he's dead but cursed to walk among the living." The exclamations of disbelief that followed this drew the attention of the campers who were on their way back from the showers. The old screen doors squeaked as the room filled up with boys holding shower caddies.

"Do Odd Otto!"

"Otto Kopp: Reduplicative Amnesia?"

"You're pronouncing it wrong," Weston said. "Long u. Reduplicative. Anyway, means he thinks there's a second version of every place on earth. He thinks there are two Mowaskins—one in Minnesota and one back home, in Ohio. He says we're in the one in Ohio."

"Santi, do Peter Van Dyke!"

He scrolled to the *V*'s. "Antisocial Personality Disorder?"

"Standard psychopath," Weston replied.

"He's a total psycho!" a boy cried cheerfully.

"Do someone in this cabin!"

Santi looked around. There was Terrence, the boy who had said they were at Mowaskin to know God. "Terry, what's your last name?"

"Dybek."

Santi found Dybek's entry. "Dolittle Phenomenon—like Dr. Dolittle?"

"Dumbest name of them all," Weston said. "No one can take it seriously. It's people who think animals talk to them. Terry says squirrels speak to him, ask him questions."

The room exploded in laughter. "What'd they ask you, Terry?" someone shouted "Where to find deez nuts?" Terrence retreated to the farthest corner of his bunk and turned to the wall. Excitement was building in the cabin and the boys pressed ever closer. "Look me up," one called from the middle of the scrum.

"Name?"

"Simon Giorgio."

Santi ran his finger down the spreadsheet. "Crapgrass Delusion?"

"Crapgrass?" someone chortled. "Simon craps in the grass!" The boys laughed and laughed but Simon's smile didn't waver. He was happy to be the focus of everyone's attention. Weston leaned over the edge of the bunk and looked at Santi, grinning. "It's Capgras, you dyslexic."

"Capgras. What's that—Capgras Delusion?"

"Shut up, monkeys!" Weston shouted. He pointed at Simon. "Hey."

"Yeah?"

"Your dad is your dad, right?" No response. "What about your mom? Or did she get replaced by an imposter, too?" The group of boys surrounding Simon opened up as they turned to look at him. Simon's whole bearing had changed. Santi thought he'd never before seen a sadder face. Weston rolled back onto his bunk. "He thinks his parents were replaced by imposters. That's Capgras. No cure."

In the loud debates that followed, Santi noticed Jude gesture to Simon to come sit next to him. He moved over to make room for the child so the other boys wouldn't see his tears. "God can cure anything," Jude said quietly.

More voices called out, asking for diagnoses. Santi went through a list of unfamiliar medical conditions, each weirder than the next— Morgellons's, Hyperempathy, Stendhal Syndrome—and told the boys the names of their illnesses while Weston explained them, but all he could think about was how he could find Jude's name in the spreadsheet without his noticing.

Suddenly, the small boy at the door hard-whispered that Counselor Dave was coming. The boys from other cabins streamed out of the cabin's side door, and those in Ezekiel's Bones returned to their bunks. "Dude, give me the phone," Weston said. Dave's heavy, oafish step was heard on the mulch trail, and now that the cabin was quieting down everyone could hear that there were two voices. Pastor Will had come to lead the Bones boys in moonlight prayers. "Jude," Weston whispered. "I'll tell." Jude threw himself on Santi and the boys wrestled over the phone.

"Tell me why you're here," Santi gasped.

"No."

The door opened and the men walked in. "What's going on here?"

Pastor Will asked. Santi released his grip on the phone. Jude slid the phone under his mattress just as the men began prying them apart.

The next morning, at breakfast, Weston's eyes were red from crying. He was telling everyone that Jude was a jerk and a fag and a liar. When Santi asked Jude what had happened, he shrugged, but Simon was thrilled to to tell someone who didn't know yet: Jude had gotten up in the middle of the night, walked out to the swimming docks, and thrown Weston's phone into Lake Mowaskin.

A WEEK LATER, Santi disappeared from camp. He was found within six hours, walking near the girls' camp across the lake. It was a little fugue, nothing like his regular ones. Almost like a hiccup. He'd known what had happened as soon as he'd stepped into the water—its touch somehow triggered a quick rebuild of the world, and the first thing he remembered was Jude. Jude had been worried, and after that he kept a very close eye on Santi. "When will you tell me?"

"I will, just not now."

"No, you won't."

"I will."

"Write it down on a piece of paper. Then I'll throw it in the campfire."

"Someone would see you."

"Then I'll eat the paper." That made Jude smile.

Santi now thought about Jude from the moment he woke up to the moment he fell asleep, when he constructed elaborate narratives featuring the two of them. These were not fantasies, because fantasies were built from the implausible. These tableaus were historical accounts, events that had already unfolded on another plane, in another place, between two people who had had possession of their hearts, because hearts were immortal, plucked from the dying and placed into those yet unborn. Santi knew they had been together many times. This love was selfish. It paid no mind to anyone or anything else, so much so that when, in the showers, Terrence cut open his wrists with Weston's jackknife, Santi could hardly spare the cost of even the smallest amount of empathy for the boy. His love demanded everything.

One day, after showers and before evening devotions, Santi was in the locker room pulling on a pair of fresh socks when Jude walked around the corner, naked and toweling off his hair. The locker room emptied. Santi picked up his shoes and moved past Jude. "I'll save you a seat."

"Wait for me."

"I don't want to be late, man."

Jude tossed him his wet towel. "Dump that in the bin for me." Santi walked the towel across the empty locker room to the dirty towel barrel. He stopped at the mirror to finger-comb his hair. "Santi."

"We gotta go."

"Come here, just for a sec."

Santi returned to the lockers. Jude was still undressed, his pale skin glistening with moisture. He stood with one foot on the old wooden bench and bent over his thigh. "Come look at this—think I should go see the nurse?"

"Stop goofing off, Jude."

"I'm serious. Look."

Reluctantly, Santi walked closer and glanced at the pink welt, averting his eyes from Jude's penis. "It's just a mosquito bite. You're such a baby." He could hear the faraway sounds of the boys singing the opening notes of "Abide with Me" by the campfire. Jude took his foot off the wooden bench and reached into his locker. "Come here." Santi shuffled a little closer. Jude placed a scrap of paper into Santi's hand. His hands trembled as he opened it. *Homosexual delusions.* Jude reached for Santi's hand and pressed it into the patchy dark hair between his legs. Santi could not move or breathe, immobilized in time as a trilobite lodged in shale. Under his fingers, he could feel Jude's body asking for something; it was the very same thing Santi's body often asked for. "This is my sickness," Jude said, his voice breaking. "And I don't want to be sick anymore."

It took great effort for Santi to speak the words because they were as sharp-edged as any truth spoken in a place of deceit and they almost hurt as they came out. "You're not sick."

"Heh," Jude said, wiping the tears from his cheek. "That's funny coming from you of all people. You and Weston, you spend all this time telling us we're sick, how they're lying about the Sickness. Now you tell me I'm not sick."

Santi couldn't think of what to say. He did not know how to explain Jude to himself.

Suddenly, Jude pushed him away with such force that Santi fell into the lockers, sending the cold metal locks swaying insanely. Jude threw himself on him, and they fell hard onto the concrete floor. They rolled around, grappling. For a while it was unclear who would prevail, but Jude eventually managed to pin Santi to the cold concrete floor, immobilizing his arms by kneeling on them.

He put his hands around Santi's throat and slammed his head against the floor. The world brightened as it did under the heat lightning of a summer storm. Santi remembered the scrap of paper in his hand. He managed to wrench his arm out from under Jude's knee and pushed the paper into his mouth. Jude froze then, or maybe the world did, but the seam, the portal that Santi loved so much, opened up and he slipped through, because that's where the pain ended.

Jude was gone now. Pastor Will and Pastor Bob and all the boys and even the camp itself. There was only the lake, and Santi was on the shore now. He saw lanterns on the water and swam out to them. The earth was patient. He knew it would outlive the lies.

"MARK"

[A man in his thirties—MARK—sits on a sofa in a sun-filled living room. Décor is upscale catalog with relatable touches, like toys on the floor, some mail on the end table. Framed family photos on the wall behind him. He is angled in such a way that we understand he's in conversation with someone off camera. As he smiles at the unseen interlocutor, an acoustic guitar strums two minor chords in succession.]

MARK: I was never someone who paid any attention to Nature. I still don't really think about it a lot. I mean, I was never the guy who went camping, or who, you know, went to the national parks and ooh'ed and ahh'ed. I can't even keep a plant alive. So it—Nature or the environment—was completely out of mind, like, not even a factor I'd consider as being part of what was happening to me.

[Mark looks down at his clasped hands. The camera pans the wall of photos. We see Mark as a teenager in wrestling gear, draped in medals; Mark celebrating a child's birthday; dressed up like a wizard for Halloween with his kids; kissing his wife.]

MARK: When I think about who I used to be, I think about a guy who had very high expectations for himself. An ambitious guy. Responsible. Used to take courses at the community college. Wrestled in high school. Got married, started a family. And I felt like everything was going right. I was on this highway to a bright future. Then this disease came and knocked me right off that highway and sent me down a dark, at times lonely, bumpy, winding, dark road.

[We cut to Mark standing in front of a mirror, staring at his reflection. There's emptiness here. V.O. (voice-over) begins.]

MARK (V.O.): All day long there is just this unrelenting exhaustion. And it doesn't matter how much I sleep. Sleep doesn't replenish it. Then I'm hit with what my wife calls ranting spells. I wouldn't even know when I'd slip into one of these states, but my family and friends would tell me that I'd been going off on some thing or another, like a crazy guy on a street corner. I never remember what I say.

[Cut back to Mark on the sofa.]

MARK: It's like disappearing from your life for a while. Scary. Then there are the depressions, which just feel impossible to get out of. And the fear, which keeps me housebound for weeks at a time. I started to develop sores on my skin with black threads that grew out of them, like my body was rotting from the inside out. Sometimes I went into fugue states. Other times I felt like I was hearing objects speaking to me or I had intense compulsions to self-harm. It's embarrassing to admit this now, but there were even times that I thought I could hear animals and even plants speaking to me, trying to get inside my head. Weird stuff. It got worse and worse. It has changed everything about me. Changed how other people look at me. I went from someone people respected to being viewed like a plague. Somewhere inside was the same person, the one with the ambitions and dreams, but now I'm trapped in this experience. I can't adapt to the Changes like other people do. And I'm becoming a burden to my family. Solastalgia—and yes, I do say the word out loud now—it's just an ugly, ugly, life-stealing disease.

[Sonic dread, in the form of a long, drawn-out violin tri-tone, begins the transition from Mark's living room to a string of images and video clips. Violent wildfires sweetened with crackling sounds

jump cut against film of massive flooding events in nondescript Midwestern towns, with people on roofs waving white pillowcases above their heads.]

NARRATOR (V.O.): In a world made strange.

[The iconic image of the St. Louis Arch knee-deep in the waters of the Mississippi cedes to public domain footage of the evacuation of Miami Beach.]

NARRATOR (V.O.): In a world defined by loss.

[Documentary stills of environmental refugees at a coastal evacuation terminal dissolve into shots of tinder-dry wheat fields, bleached reefs, and dead forests.]

NARRATOR (V.O.): In a world that makes hope hard to come by . . . Climafeel can help.

[Music transitions to cheerful major chords and the imagery shifts: a family picnicking; a couple gazing at each other over a candlelit dinner; cheerful teenagers on skateboards.]

NARRATOR (V.O.): Developed with you in mind, Climafeel offers the Impacted an opportunity to face their changing world with fearlessness and stress immunity while retaining the emotional versatility needed to experience optimism, affection, unparalleled focus, and productivity. Vortex's world-class geneticists have developed a safe and effective treatment for solastalgia that eliminates fragility, polishes awareness, and offers anxiety-free living in our challenging circumstances. Seamless adaptation *is* possible with Climafeel.

[We are back in Mark's living room, but he is now surrounded by his family—his wife and two young children. He snuggles one child under each arm.]

MARK: Climafeel? It's given me my life back. It's made me a better parent and a better partner because I'm present. I'm engaged. I see a future and a way forward. Don't get me wrong, I still care about what's happening out there. I still care about the world. I know we've got some problems to solve. But with Climafeel, my caring and my concern don't make me sick. I'm able to tolerate the Changes instead of being broken by them. We all know that broken people can't help anyone. And I want to help, because I do care. I care a lot. But I care on my terms.

[Cut to Mark and his kids playing in the backyard.]

NARRATOR (V.O.): Climafeel is a recombinant DNA biologic that blunts the effects of solastalgia, utilizing the genetically modified Taq1 A1 allele on the ANKK1 gene, which is related to Cleckley's Syndrome.

[text on screen] Climafeel is not approved for use in elderly patients experiencing retroactive climate change denial, as it may make these symptoms worse.

NARRATOR (V.O.): A temporary reduction in the ability to appreciate visual art, theater, and music may occur. Brief periods of low empathy have been seen in some people. If these periods persist, speak to your doctor.

[text on screen] Symptom severity should be high to indicate the use of Climafeel in children. Parents should talk to their pediatrician about the risks and benefits.

NARRATOR (V.O.): You should report persistent low empathy, homicidal thoughts, prolonged absence of remorse, and disinhibition that results in legal problems.

[text on screen] You and your doctor should also monitor, discuss, and report any adverse events if they occur. Please see the drug insert for a complete list of possible side effects.

[Mark and his children are shooting hoops in the driveway as his wife looks on. He lifts one child up and helps her to dunk the ball.]

NARRATOR (V.O.): *We may not be able to put the world back together, but Climafeel can make it easier to be in the world. Ask your doctor if Climafeel is right for you.*

Acknowledgments

In 2005, environmental philosopher Glenn Albrecht coined the term *solastalgia* to describe the specific kind of grief human beings experience as the natural world changes around them. He calls it "the homesickness you have while you are still at home." It's grief that anticipates a separation, perhaps a final one, while you are still in the place you know you will leave. Or lose.
Albrecht's brilliant neologism haunts and disturbs me, perhaps because I recognize it in myself. In these pages I've processed his concept by imagining solastalgia into an illness the world tries to cure, a disease to be eliminated, a mental illness to be treated. But grief is not pathological. It is the inevitable endpoint of love. Solastalgia exists because we love Nature, and as long as we still love Nature, there is hope for us. I want to express my great gratitude to Dr. Albrecht for his body of work.

I have been exceedingly lucky to have been given opportunities by a number of literary journals, magazines, and publishers to publish some of these strange tales, including Radix Media, *Hotel Amerika, KYSO Flash, Audubon Magazine,* Alternating Current, *Arcturus/The Chicago Review of Books,* and *Enizagam.*

It is my great privilege to be in the University of Minnesota Press family. My editor, Erik Anderson, is a deeply perceptive and uncommonly creative thinker and artist. He saw the architecture of this collection long before I did, and his skilled and sensitive editing improved these pages immeasurably. As we worked on revisions, and I floundered in the "madness stage" of the process, Erik told me, "The ship is far out to sea, we haven't seen land for a while, the rations are getting repetitive, and that bright lunacy is setting in." Every writer, particularly those who "write weird," deserves a reader like Erik.

It has also been my privilege to work with a number of intelligent and thoughtful folks at the University of Minnesota Press, including

Shelby Connelly, Rachel Moeller, Jeff Moen, Emma Saks, Maggie Sattler, Heather Skinner, Matt Smiley, and Laura Westlund. Louisa Castner's perceptive copy editing improved these pages significantly and saved me from many minor and major embarrassments.

A number of professors and teachers have considered *South Pole Station* and "Muri" worthy of inclusion in their climate change or climate fiction course syllabi or as topics of conference talks or panel discussions. I'm grateful for their commitment to exploring with young people—on their own terms—the impact of climate change on Nature, humanity, and the individual. Your work is profoundly important.

As always, thanks are due to three brilliant women: Dr. Starr Sage, Delta Larkey, and Lacy Shelby, all of whom spend their time making this world a better place. My parents, Don and Barbara Shelby, are always game for whatever I'm laying down, even mutinous polar bears. Jason Albert read countless pages of garbage as I grappled with my own solastalgia while writing these stories. I don't know why Jeff Meredith always seems to show up in my books, but he does, and I'm glad he's there. Alex DiFrancesco is a generous soul and a gifted writer, and their words of support buoyed me at a time I was adrift. The extraordinary writer Omar El Akkad not only made time to read these pages, he also read what was in my heart. It is a kindness I did nothing to deserve but for which I'm deeply grateful.

Hudson, Joey, and Manny: another one. I could not do these sorts of things without your love, support, and tolerance for my general and specific weirdness.

One final acknowledgment: to young people. I'm sorry for what you have been asked to carry. This should not be your burden. But you do not live alone in what Aldo Leopold called "this world of wounds." You have already shown that you have the courage to see what many of those older than you would not and still will not. Your love of this planet—along with your rage, your fear, your grief, and your ideas—is powerful enough to bind its wounds, one at a time. Above all, safeguard hope. Ignore those who say it doesn't exist. They're wrong. Hope is everywhere, for those who search for spring.

Publication History

Stories in this collection, some in different form, were originally published in the following publications.

"Muri" was first published by Radix Media in its Futures Science Fiction series.

"Honeymoons in Temporary Locations" was published in *Arcturus/The Chicago Review of Books*.

"Post-Impact Craigslist Ads"; "Impact Cruises' Brochure Text: 'Endangered Cities 7-Day Free-Sail Cruise'"; "Unicorn Investments Newsletter: Subscription Confirmation E-mail"; and "Three Rivers Park District Class Description: 'New Friends at the Feeder'" were published collectively as "Emergent Norm Theory and Post-Climate Change Impact: Appendix A" in *Enizagam*.

"Federal Eligibility Questionnaire from the Temporary Aid to Climate-Impacted Deserving Poor Benefits Program" was published as "Eligibility Questionnaire: Temporary Aid to Climate-Impacted Deserving Poor Benefits Program" in *High Shelf*.

"Ersatz Café Menu (Store #350)" was published as "Ersatz Café's Post-Climate Impact Menu" in *KYSO Flash*.

"Violent Biophilia in Solastalgia Patients: Case Study" was published as "Case Study: Violent Biophilia in Solastalgia Patients" in *Hotel Amerika*.

"The Ingenious Futility of Warblers (Elizabeth Fugit)" was published in *Audubon Magazine*.

Ashley Shelby is a novelist, short story writer, and former environmental journalist. Her debut novel *South Pole Station* was a *New York Times* Editors' Pick and winner of the Lascaux Prize in Fiction. She is the author of *Red River Rising: The Anatomy of a Flood and the Survival of an American City,* and her writing has been published in the *New York Times, LitHub, Salon, Audubon,* and *The Nation.* She lives in the Twin Cities.